DETOUR

A POST-APOCALYPTIC HORROR STORY

G. MICHAEL HOPF

Copyright © 2018 G. Michael Hopf
No part of this book may be reproduced in any manner whatsoever without permission except in the case of brief quotations embodied in critical articles or reviews.
For information contact:
geoff@gmichaelhopf.com
www.gmichaelhopf.com
All rights reserved.
ISBN-13: 78-1725050037
ISBN-10: 172505003X

DEDICATION

TO SAVANNAH

"The boundaries which divide Life from Death are at best shadowy and vague. Who shall say where the one ends, and where the other begins?"

- Edgar Allen Poe

PROLOGUE

AUSCHWITZ, GERMAN-OCCUPIED POLAND

JANUARY 13, 1945

Dr. Josef Clauberg knew the end was coming, and fast the second he heard the first Soviet artillery smashing into the German lines miles away. The reports flooding into their headquarters at the concentration camp were that the German army would hold the Russian advance, but Clauberg knew otherwise. After the Allied invasion in Normandy six months before, he had begun to prepare for his departure by making arrangements and creating a false identification.

Dr. Erich Clucks, his protégé and assistant for the past four years, burst through the front door. "It worked, Herr Doctor, it worked!"

Clauberg looked up from a box he was packing and asked, "It did?"

"Yes, Doctor, come, hurry!" Erich exclaimed, sweat streaming down his face.

The thumping of artillery echoed in the distance.

Erich looked out the smudged windows of Clauberg's office and barked, "Doctor, we don't have much time!" Erich turned and sprinted out of the office.

Clauberg dropped what he was doing and followed.

The two raced through darkened hallways until they entered a ward of the hospital kept under heavy security.

Down the hall, Erich and Clauberg ran until they reached the last room on the right.

Clauberg paused before going inside. "Are you sure it worked?"

"Doctor, it did. This could help us in the war; we must get this information to the Fuhrer," Erich exclaimed.

"Erich, the war is lost. We must look to ourselves now," Clauberg said, touching Erich's shoulder.

"But, Doctor…" Erich said, shocked by Clauberg's words.

"Go to your office and gather your things. We're leaving today," Clauberg ordered.

"Doctor, I don't understand," Erich said, bewildered. "The German high command says the Soviets will be turned back before they arrive."

"Lies, it's all lies. The war was over the second the Americans landed in France. Now go, hurry, get your things and meet me at my office in fifteen minutes," Clauberg said.

"But, Doctor—" Erich said, standing frozen in dismay.

"Go!" Clauberg barked.

Frightened, Erich turned and ran off.

Clauberg watched until Erich had disappeared. He opened the door and entered the examination room to find a woman chained to the wall. She was seething with anger and foaming at the mouth. "How are you?"

The woman charged at him but only got within a few feet of him before the chain went taut, causing her to fall backwards onto her back. She jumped to her feet and charged again.

Clauberg folded his arms. A tear formed in the corner of his eye. It had worked; he had done it. "You're marvelous," he said, pulling out his sidearm, a Luger P08 pistol. He slid the slide back, chambered a round, and leveled it at the woman's head.

Once more, she ran at him with all her might, and once again, the chain proved too much. She fell back and landed on her butt.

Clauberg aimed his pistol and squeezed the trigger. The nine-millimeter round struck her in the forehead and blew out the back of her head.

She slumped forward dead, blood pouring out of the gaping wound in the back of her skull.

Clauberg holstered the pistol, ran to a side table, grabbed several syringes with vials and added anticoagulant to them, then went to the woman's dead body. He injected the needle into the woman's arm and drew blood until the vial was full. He repeated this several more times. When he was done, he placed the syringes into a leather satchel on the table and cinched it closed. He went to leave but stopped a foot from the door. He turned around, looked at the body of the woman, and said, "Thank you for your contribution."

***

Back at his office, Clauberg found Erich waiting, a box in his arms.

"It was as I said, correct, Doctor?" Erich asked.

"It was, Erich, it was. Now do me a favor and call Obersoldat Heinz. Tell him I'm ready to leave," Clauberg ordered.

Erich didn't hesitate like before. He walked to the phone on the desk, picked it up, and dialed a single digit. The phone connected promptly.

"Yes, Herr Doctor," Heinz answered.

"This is Dr. Clucks. Dr. Clauberg wishes to be picked up now," Erich said.

"Yes, sir," Heinz said then hung up.

"He's coming," Erich said.

"Good," Clauberg said, hastily packing the last few items he needed, which included the satchel with the syringes.

A horn sounded outside.

"Time to go," Clauberg said, picking up his box and rushing from his office with Erich close behind.

The two exited the building just as a succession of heavy artillery sounded. This time it was closer than before.

"That sounded like—" Erich said, loading his box into the car.

"Soon the Soviets will be here. No time to waste," Clauberg said, climbing into the backseat of the car, his box cradled in his arms.

Erich got in next to him, his face displaying the fear and trepidation of the situation. "Are we abandoning our posts, Doctor?"

Heinz looked over his shoulder and asked, "Herr

Doctor, are you ready?"

"Drive," Clauberg barked. He looked at Erich and said, "Technically yes, but soon there won't be a Nazi government or army that can prosecute us."

The car sped off and out a rear gate that had been left open per Clauberg's instructions.

"What about our years of work?" Erich asked.

"I saved it. In this bag I have her blood, and with it we can continue our work. Oh, she was perfect, she responded as we hoped; our only problem is time."

"What will we do with it?" Erich asked.

Clauberg opened the satchel and removed a syringe. He held it up, admiring the blood that was contained in the glass vial. "We have lost this war, but with this we will live to fight another day."

Erich gave Clauberg an awkward smile and asked, "Doctor, where are we going?"

"To South America, I have friends there."

CHAPTER ONE

NEW YORK, NEW YORK

MAY 25, 2020

Natalie Atkinson was never a woman to shy away from challenges and had always taken pride in the fact she was always ready to take risks. She liked to claim it was this part of her personality that made her a successful dealer and purveyor of rare items and antiquities. She was one of the most sought after in her field, and it was because if given a job and the price was right, she'd find whatever someone wanted.

She approached the front doors of the restaurant but couldn't find the strength to take her inside. She'd never found herself so undecided, but here she was unable to cross the threshold and close the deal.

"Is this right?" she asked herself, pacing back and forth.

Passersby ogled her as she talked loudly to herself, her hands and arms motioning as she talked.

"Ma'am, are you Ms. Atkinson?" the maître d' from the restaurant asked sheepishly.

"Ah, yes, I'm her," she replied, her eyes wide with panic.

"A gentleman asked that I come tell you that he's waiting for you," he said.

"Oh, yes, of course," she said. "I'll be right in,

sorry."

"Shall I escort you to the table, or will you be longer?" he asked.

"Um, well..." she answered. Catching that her tone and appearance seemed out of sorts, she was determined to remedy the problem. Standing tall and exhaling deeply, she continued, "You may escort me to the table, thank you."

"This way, ma'am," the maître d said, motioning with his arm to the front door.

She followed him through the dimly lit restaurant. The rich and savory aroma of meat filled the air. The distinct clang of crystal wineglasses and laughter sounded from the back of the restaurant, causing her to turn to see a small group of people celebrating. Was it a birthday? Or maybe an engagement? she wondered. The walk to her table was like a maze, but instead of tall shrubs, she navigated past small tables with pristine white tablecloths.

At the very back of the restaurant sat a single table nestled in a leather booth. A man scooted out and stood awaiting her arrival.

Natalie approached cautiously. In front of her was a man who would forever change her life, yet she'd never formally met him before.

"My dear Natalie, so nice of you to come," the man said, holding out his hand.

Natalie smiled and took his hand. "Nice to finally meet you, James."

James' body was tall and muscular. Odd for someone who clearly looked as if he was in his mid to late sixties, maybe even seventy if she were to guess. "Please sit down," James said.

"Thank you," Natalie said, sliding into the booth.

James sat on the opposite side of the table and smiled.

The maître d' stepped forward and said, "A waiter will be here shortly to serve you."

Natalie smiled.

James didn't even look at the maître d'; his attention was fully on Natalie.

The maître d' walked off, leaving them alone.

"You're late," James said abruptly, his polite tone quickly changing. "I called, no answer. I texted, nothing. I finally was heading to the front when I saw you out front pacing back and forth. Is everything okay?"

Ashamed of her behavior and tardiness, she said, "I apologize, but after what I went through to get this, I'm going to have to change the terms of the deal."

"What does that mean?" James asked, annoyed. He hated last minute alterations of business arrangements. He always found them to be a distasteful way of doing business, specifically if the person asking for the change had leverage.

"I need an additional two hundred thousand for the trouble—legal, mind you—I went through in Argentina."

He'd had a feeling it was concerning money. Normally he would have scoffed, in his business life he would have thrown the person out, but this was personal, deeply personal. "Fine."

"You'll pay the additional amount to cover my

troubles?" she asked, amazed that he agreed so easily. She then wondered if she went too cheap.

"So, are you ready to do business?" James asked.

Natalie pressed her eyes closed tightly for a brief second, opened them and said, "Yes, let's do this."

A waiter approached, "Good evening, my name is Steven. I'll be serving you tonight. Can I start you off with a drink?"

Taking charge, James said, "A bottle of Dom, please."

"Two glasses?" the waiter asked.

Natalie nodded. "Yes, please."

"Very well, I'll be right back," the waiter said and rushed off.

"Dom is very nice," Natalie said.

"I think there's reason to celebrate," James said, his tone shifting back to jovial.

The two exchanged small talk until the waiter returned with the bottle of champagne. Once they each had a glass, James said, "Here's to finding rare and special things."

Natalie touched his glass with hers and smiled. "Yes." Natalie was always amazed by what collectors found valuable; some people would consider things trash, and others would see a thing of beauty.

The two sipped their drinks; then James got down to business.

"Do you have it?" James asked.

"I do," Natalie said, nodding.

"I'll just trust that it's the real thing," James said, his

anxiety rising.

"It's real, that I can tell you. I know my business, as I suspect you know yours," Natalie replied.

"Can I see it?" James asked, his demeanor turning to that of a child.

She reached into her large handbag and removed a hard case. She unfastened a latch and opened the box to reveal three large vials of thick dark blood sitting nestled in dry ice. "Here it is," she said, sliding it across the table to James.

James snatched it, his eyes wide with pure ecstasy. "It looks as if it were drawn just yesterday."

Natalie smiled. She never understood people's fascination with certain objects, and tried never to judge, but she was curious about it. "What's the full story?"

"I don't want to bore you, and if I did, you might find it a bit unsavory," he replied. "When you said it had been discovered in a refrigerated storage facility in Argentina, I was thrilled and doubtful. Fortunately few even know about it, as Dr. Clauberg died shortly after arriving in Buenos Aires," he said, his eyes fixed on the vials. He looked up at her and asked, "Can I touch it?"

She reached across the table, pulled the box back towards her, and closed the lid. "Not yet. When you make the transfer, then you can have it."

James removed his mobile phone, sent a text, then put it back in his pocket.

The waiter returned. He took their dinner order and left.

"What will you do with the money?" James asked.

"First thing I'm doing is taking a vacation. I've got a nice spot picked out, a quiet place."

"Where?" he asked.

With a sweet smile she answered, "That's none of your business."

"Fair enough," he said, returning the smile. "I have to say, you are what they say you are."

"And what's that?" she quipped.

He folded his hands and answered, "As you know, I'm a collector of the unique, and after reading through some journals I had gotten at an auction, I was curious if the blood still existed. I imagined it didn't, but I needed to know, I had to know. I asked around, I have good contacts, and your name came back several times."

"And what do they say about me?" she asked.

"That you're expensive." He laughed. "And that you always find what someone is looking for."

"I pride myself on it. It takes time, like this did, but it eventually showed up. I'll say that I met some interesting characters along the way too," she said.

"I bet you did," he said. "You said you had to do some things that were, how did you put it?"

"Unethical," she said, answering his question to her.

"What was that? I seemed to have paid for this unethical behavior; I have a right to know," he asked, curious.

"When I found it, word somehow got out, and the local authorities decided they wanted to seize it due to its historical significance. I had to grease some hands—you have to love Latin countries, graft and bribery are ways of doing business—but I got it back, and now it's right here," she said, tapping the top of the box.

"That was it?" he asked, confused, thinking the story would be fraught with agony, pain, something more than bribing a few people.

"Does spending two nights in a Buenos Aires jail sound fun? Or that I was groped but before making the final deal. Then to top it all off, they wanted to sell each one by themselves. In the end I stole the other two and got out of the country before I could be arrested again."

"Then I do owe you for your troubles. I'm sorry that happened to you, and I'm grateful that you worked so hard to get it," he said.

The waiter returned with their meals and set them down. "Can I get you anything else?"

"No, and I'll take the check now," James replied, anxious to get his hands on the box.

The two ate their meals. They kept the conversation to small talk until they were finished.

"I assume you have a way to check your account online?" James asked.

"Has the money gone through?" Natalie asked.

"I suggest you check," James said, grinning.

Natalie snatched her phone from her handbag and went directly to an app for a bank in Switzerland she had for deals such as these. She logged in and waited. Seconds later on her screen she saw the number they had agreed upon. "It's there."

"It is. Now the box," James said, leaning forward.

She pushed the box over.

James grabbed it and held it as if he were holding the most precious thing in the world.

Natalie smiled. It was satisfying to have a job come to an end and a happy client. "I suppose you'll want to get it home and tucked into whatever display case you have."

"I do have a nice place for it," he said as his hand caressed the top of the box.

She scooted out of the booth and said, "It was a pleasure doing business with you."

James looked up and said, "I'll be in touch soon, I suppose. I have some other items from that era I'm looking for."

"You know how to reach me," Natalie said.

James got out of the booth with the box cradled in his hands. "Goodbye, Natalie," he said and walked off.

GREENWICH, CONNECTICUT

James rushed to his basement without uttering a word to his wife, Tiffany. He unlocked a heavy door, flipped on a few lights, and entered the large space. The room was immense. It spanned the length and width of the main house footprint. Along the walls stood display cases and shelves, all full of items, large and small. This was more a museum than anything else. To an average person they'd nod and look but would find many of the items distasteful or more fitting in a real museum, the reason being James' collection wasn't just any odd, priceless or unique items; it was World War Two memorabilia, specifically artifacts from Nazi Germany and some of Adolf Hitler's personal effects.

His collection started not long after discovering who his birth parents were. On his eighteenth birthday, the people he thought were his parents didn't give him a car or a paid trip to somewhere fun; no, they sat him down and gave him the news that he had been adopted. This was where his journey for all things Nazi had begun. Using what little information he had been given, he ended up finding out that his birth parents were from Germany and both had died in the fire bombings of Dresden in 1945. He had miraculously survived the attack and had been sent to an orphanage, where he was promptly adopted by an American family and brought to live in New Hampshire.

After discovering his true identity and lineage, he came to find out that his birth father was a ranking member in the Nazi party and had at one time been a close confidant to Hitler himself. Fascinated, he wanted to know more. This fascination turned into obsession as he began to collect whatever artifacts he could get his hands on. He kept his hobby and enthusiasm with Nazi Germany primarily to himself, but over the years he'd found a group of others who shared his appreciation. These weren't skinheads or neo-Nazis; he found those types repugnant. Instead he chose to surround himself with what he called intellectuals, these were people who appreciated the old regime and could defend or debate its archaic and evil policies aptly by applying science and data. He grew fond of his group of friends, many of them being invited to his house so he could share with them the items he had found and purchased.

His collection exploded when his business became highly successful, enabling him to buy rarer and sometimes elusive items. What ultimately led him to being in possession of the vials started when he had acquired the journals of Dr. Clauberg at an auction. Few people had ever heard of the Nazi doctor; his notoriety had never reached the levels of some, specifically Dr. Mengele. However, James was a student of all things Nazi Germany and had come across Clauberg's name while doing some sourced research. So when he had heard that Clauberg's journals were up for auction, he went to go get them, no matter the price. After securing the journals, he pored over them, reading every word. Clauberg had kept meticulous notes and referenced the vials in a postscript dated January 1945. That was it for James. If the vials still existed, he wanted them. They were one of a kind, a find that for him was priceless. He sought out a person who could track them down, which led to Natalie. The rest was history.

He darted for a small case in the far corner of the basement. He set the box on a table next to it, removed a set of keys from his pocket, and unlocked the glass door. He opened it and gave a thermostat a glance to ensure the temperature was where it needed to be. If he was going to preserve the contents of the vials, he would have to keep them stored in a climate-controlled and refrigerated case. Using his connections, he had had a man retrofit a wine refrigerator with glass shelves and added UV protection to the thick glass door. On the center shelf inside, he had made a cradle for the vials. This would protect them yet beautifully display the vials.

Filled with excitement that his moment had come, he unlocked the box and carefully removed the first vial. He looked at it closely, taking in every detail no matter how small. He imagined Clauberg holding the vial. Oh, the joy he felt holding something that a man like Clauberg once touched.

He set the first vial inside the cradle, then took the second and repeated what he did with the first. He took the third in his hand and examined it. He held it upside down, watching the blood flow. The next best thing would be to touch it, but he knew that would ruin his rare find.

"James, what do you have there?" Tiffany called out from the doorway.

Startled, James dropped the vial. It fell to the hardwood floor and smashed into hundreds of pieces. The blood splattered on the display case and his pants. "Damn it!"

"Oh no," Tiffany said, coming to his aid.

He crouched down and looked at the shattered glass on the floor, tears coming to his eyes.

Tiffany came up behind him and touched his shoulder. "Let me help."

He shrugged her hand off his shoulder and snapped, "Look at what you did!"

"Me? I didn't do anything," she said, defending herself.

"You came in here unannounced and gave me a fright; now this most precious item is destroyed!" he bellowed.

"Is that blood?" she asked.

He whipped his head back and yelled, "Leave, go, get out of here!"

Placing her hands on her hips, she said, "Sometimes I hate you, you know that?"

"Leave now!" he cried out in anger, the sight of the destroyed vial bringing him to tears.

Doing as he asked, she turned and stormed off and went back upstairs.

James knelt and stared at the blood and glass. He thought about what he could do. Maybe he could scoop it up and place it in another vessel. He looked around but saw nothing. Distraught, he came to the realization that this vial was gone for good. No matter what he did, the value of it was zero, but he did have two more, he thought.

He recalled wanting to touch the blood, and now he could. If he had to throw this away, he'd at least get some value from the accident. He reached down with his index finger and touched the cool thick blood. He raised his hand and stared at it. He put his other fingers together and began to rub the blood between his fingertips. He lowered his other hand so he could get more blood. When he touched it, a sliver of glass cut his finger.

"Ouch," he said and recoiled. He looked at the finger. The blood of Mother and his blood were mixing. A tinge of fear ran through him. Had he just become contaminated? He recalled reading in Clauberg's journals about how the blood came to be and the experiments. Would he become like the woman?

His fear grew. He stood up and ran to the bathroom. There he turned on the faucet and ran his cut finger under the running water. Using a bar of soap, he began to feverishly wash the cut and his entire hand.

After spending minutes washing, he stopped. He still felt fine; according to the journals, he would start to display symptoms. Maybe the blood was so old the chemical compounds from the serum were degraded and basically inert. He glanced at his reflection in the mirror above the sink and said, "You're a damn fool."

He toweled off his hands, blood slowly oozing from the cut. He opened the medicine cabinet, found antibiotic ointment and dabbed a small amount on, then placed a Band-Aid over the cut. "There, all better," he said out loud.

He exited the bathroom and looked over at the refrigerated display to see the door was open. He walked over, closed and locked it. He glanced at the floor and shrugged. "I'll clean you up tomorrow," he said, a tone of disgust in his voice. What had begun as one of the most exciting evenings of his life had ended terribly. Tired and ready for bed, he headed up the stairs to go to sleep.

***

James woke abruptly, his stomach was churning, and his body ached horribly. He glanced at the clock and saw he'd been asleep for just over three hours. His head was spinning, and the urge to urinate was overwhelming. He climbed out of bed and headed to the bathroom. As he took the last step inside the bathroom, a surge of adrenaline hit him. "Whoa," he said out loud, shocked by the rush; then another bolt of adrenaline raced through his body, this time more intense. "Oh no." Fear rippled through him, as he'd never felt anything like that before, and he knew it had to do with the blood. His fear turned to panic after the third surge, this one topping the other two. An immeasurable thirst suddenly came over him.

He stepped out of the bathroom and walked to the kitchen, heading directly for the refrigerator. He pulled the handle on the refrigerator so hard he nearly broke it. With the refrigerator open, the smells and aromas from everything hit him; it was as if his sense of smell was heightened. A ravenous hunger suddenly appeared. However, the only thing he desired was meat…raw and bloody meat. He tore through the lower drawers until he found a packet of ground beef. He ripped it open and began to shove it into his mouth. On the top shelf he saw a gallon of milk. He tore the top off and began to guzzle, but it wasn't enough. His hunger only grew.

Blood began to drip from his face and onto his arms, chest and legs. He touched it, curious as to what was bleeding. He raced to the closest mirror and saw his nose was bleeding. The blood gave off a scent, something he'd never smelled before. He wiped his nose with his hand then licked the blood from it. It was then that he found the taste of blood to be intoxicating.

"James, what are you doing?" Tiffany asked.

His eyes widened when he heard her. He spun around and stared.

"Honey, are you alright? You're bleeding," she said, walking towards him.

He tried to speak but found it hard to make out a word. It was as if he'd forgotten how to.

She walked up close and examined him. "Sweetheart, are you hurt? You're bleeding badly from your nose."

All he could see were the veins in her neck pulsating, the blood coursing through. His hunger had reached epic proportions, and all he could think about was feeding on her.

"Let me get you cleaned up," she said, taking his hand.

The touch of her hand felt almost erotic in a way. His senses were at a level unknown to him; touch, smell, hearing and taste were all elevated.

She tried to move him, but he stood frozen to the spot, his dilated eyes staring at her.

"James, you're scaring me," she said.

He heard the name James but now couldn't recall who that was or who she was. It was as if his memory was being replaced with a primal desire and hunger to kill and eat.

"Why are you looking at me that way?" she said, letting go of his hand and stepping back.

Before she could take another step, his instincts kicked in. He grabbed her, drew her close, and bit into her neck as a vampire would with an open mouth. He pulled back and tore away a large chunk of flesh from her throat.

Blood spurted from the wound. She gasped and tried again to pull away but found his grip too tight.

Again he brought her in and bit down, this time going deeper into the same spot.

She wailed in pain before fainting.

Giving in to his hunger, he fed on her, biting different parts and ripping away the flesh. He'd chew but mainly swallowed. Her blood dripped down from his mouth, covering his torso. When he had his fill, he left what remained of her on the floor, surrounded by a pool of blood and flesh.

Outside, he heard a car drive up slowly. It was the newspaper being delivered.

He ran to a large window that overlooked the street. Staring out at the streetlights, he was amazed by what he saw. It was as if he'd never seen it before.

The driver tossed a paper and sped off.

Needing to be set free and explore, he did what felt natural. Using his newfound strength, he leapt through the window. With a thud, he landed on his feet. Like a wild animal, he shook off the glass and peered down the street, looking for the rear lights of the deliveryman. Seeing the car slow two houses down, James sprinted towards him. He reached him quickly and grabbed the driver's left arm. The man fought back and got his arm free but not before James had bitten him.

The driver hit the accelerator and sped off before James could do further damage. Looking at the bleeding wound on his arm, the driver headed towards the closest hospital.

Angered by his inability to get the driver, James looked around and headed towards the house in front of him.

When the sun rose six hours later, James had killed eighteen people and wounded another twenty-three before being gunned down by police.

CHAPTER TWO

SALT LAKE CITY, UTAH

MAY 30, 2020

Kevin was finding it hard to focus on cooking with the television in the living room blaring nonstop about a virus or sickness that was spreading, coupled with sudden outbreaks of violence in many cities.

"Honey, can you turn that down?" Kevin hollered, his attention on the blade of his knife as it slid through a juicy beefsteak tomato.

"Kev, you need to come see this!" Megan cried out. "They say it's getting worse, like the government might start calling for evacuations of Kansas City, even Los Angeles. You should see some of the footage."

"I don't have time. Plus you need to remember the news isn't the news anymore, it's entertainment, and their business model is structured around advertising. They get you clicking and waiting through the ads on TV by having sensational stuff."

Megan was curled up on the couch, her legs pulled in tight, her eyes fixed on the prerecorded footage of a suspected infected person attacking others outside a hospital. "Oh my God! Kev, please come see this! This is just like what I saw on my way home from work today."

"I said I can't, unless you don't want my world-famous caprese," Kevin said, pulling a ball of fresh mozzarella from the refrigerator.

"Jesus, what was that?" Megan screamed from the other room. She jumped up from her comfortable nest and ran to the kitchen. "No, Kev, you need to see this. It's just how I described what I saw earlier today."

Frustrated, Kevin put the knife down and said, "If I go and take a look, will you promise you won't bother me again, so I can finish dinner?"

"Promise, now come," Megan said, grabbing his arm and dragging him from the kitchen. She pulled him to the couch and turned up the television volume. "They're going to replay it. Just be patient."

Kevin stood, his arms crossed and fingers tapping. "I'm waiting."

She nudged him and said, "Be patient."

The news replayed the clip of a man attacking others at the entrance of a hospital before being shot down by police.

"That was it?" Kevin asked, not impressed.

"They say the man came in 'cause he'd been bitten by a person who attacked him hours earlier. Did you see that? It's like he has rabies or something," Megan said.

"Are you saying these people are all infected with rabies? I think this is all a bunch of BS. The media needs you glued to the television so they can sell ad space. Remember, Meg, I'm in advertising sales; this is what I do."

"Maybe they're some sort of zombies," Megan blurted out.

"Zombies? Really? Okay, that's enough television for one night," Kevin said, picking up the remote and turning off the television.

"No!" Megan protested.

"Meg, I'm making our special dinner, I took off work to do this, and you're in here watching nonsense and saying zombies or people with rabies are attacking other people in the street. Come into the kitchen with me, open a bottle of wine, and let's enjoy the night," Kevin said, taking her arm and coaxing her towards the kitchen.

Her annoyance with him melted away as she remembered the night was to celebrate their being together for a year. "You're right, I'm sorry. It's just that stuff is scary. The news is saying…plus I know what I saw."

"I said it already, the news isn't news. They're companies structured around selling advertising, and they're no different than scripted shows. Ever notice how they'll tell you about a story, give you a juicy bit, then have you wait until the end of the segment to play it, and it ends up being nothing at all, but you suffered through boring car or laundry detergent commercials."

"I know they need to sell ads, but—"

"Meg, I'm in advertising; I know what I'm talking about. Now come, let's enjoy our evening, and that includes keeping your phone off," Kevin said, taking her phone and turning it off. "Tonight you're mine."

"But what if someone needs to get in touch with me?" she said, finding it hard to detach from her phone.

"Who?" he asked, brow furrowed, waiting for a

plausible excuse, which he knew didn't exist.

"Paul might need something," she said.

"Paul is a grown man. He'll be fine for one night."

"Are you sure?" she asked.

"Positive. I don't want our night to be interrupted. Plus it's not like the world is going to end tonight. Whoever needs us can reach us tomorrow," he said, taking his phone and turning it off as well.

***

Megan rolled over and caressed Kevin's chest. "Thank you for the dinner and the dessert," she purred.

"My pleasure," he quipped.

Megan suddenly went quiet.

After a long pause, Kevin asked, "What is it?"

"Nothing."

"I know you, something is wrong," Kevin said, nudging her.

"It's nothing, I swear," she said, rolling onto her back. She stared at the ceiling, deep in thought.

Kevin propped himself up on his elbow and said, "When a woman says *nothing*, it means *something*."

"Do you love me?" she asked.

"Of course I love you," he replied.

She again fell silent.

"Meg, what's wrong? Have I said or done something? Was it because I turned off your phone?"

"If we get married, I'm not saying we will, but if we do, will you promise to take care of Paul?" she asked, referring to her younger brother.

"Take care of Paul? I don't understand," Kevin said, sitting up, his back against the headboard.

Megan followed suit, her hands folded on her lap. "You know Paul, he's...oh, how do I say it? He just needs help."

"He's just slower than others, but I think he's done a good job settling in at the video game store. He really seems to like it."

"Ever since he was little, he's been different. Then after my parents died, I've had to step up and be his mother and father. He needs someone like you to help him through tough times, as I may not always be around."

"Damn the news," Kevin growled.

"Why would you say that?"

"You're worried that this crap on the news is going to kill you, and now you're having life-and-death thoughts cross your mind."

"It's not that, I swear," she said, tucking a strand of her long blond hair behind her ear. "We've been together for a year now, and if you ask me, I think we might be headed towards the big M word, and I wanted you to know that I'm a package deal. You marry me, you get my brother too."

Kevin took in everything she said and thought. She was serious, more so than he'd ever seen her. He wasn't opposed to such conversations; he just hadn't expected it tonight.

"Now you're quiet," Megan said, her gaze fixed on

him.

"You hit me with a lot. To be honest, I thought tonight would be just good food, great sex and fun conversation."

"Sorry I destroyed your evening," Megan moped.

"You didn't destroy anything; I'm just taking it all in. You kind of hit me with a ton to think about."

"So you need time?" Megan asked.

He turned, faced her and said, "I don't need time to think about how much I love you and that I too have been thinking about marriage. I see us together for a long time, but when you said the thing about taking care of Paul, are you meaning financially? Like one day he could come live with us?"

"He might. You never know what life throws at you," Megan answered.

He pondered her comment and said, "I love you, Megan, with or without Paul. And if you're a package deal, then I take the entire package. If one day we're to become a family, then Paul is also my family."

"So you promise to take care of him, no matter what, treat him like a brother and a son when he needs that type of support?"

"I do."

She leaned in, wrapped her arms tightly around him, and squeezed. "I love you."

"I love you too."

CHAPTER THREE

SALT LAKE CITY, UTAH

MAY 31, 2020

Loud banging on the front door woke Kevin first, followed by Megan, who opened her eyes and mumbled something unintelligible.

Kevin sat up and looked at a still-drowsy Megan. "Who do you suppose that is?"

Megan reached for her phone, which normally sat on the nightstand but wasn't there. "My phone is in the kitchen and off."

"Mine's in there too," Kevin said, dragging himself out of bed. He slipped on a pair of shorts and a T-shirt and headed to the front door.

The banging on the front door continued.

"Hold on, hold on!" Kevin hollered. He reached the front door and peeked through the peephole to find Paul there. He sighed loudly then unlocked the door. When he opened it, Paul raced in.

"I thought you two were dead or worse," Paul said, panting, his large belly heaving with each step and breath he took.

"What can be worse than dead?" Kevin said, slamming the door.

Sirens blared in the distance, but Kevin ignored

them, not thinking anything of it.

"They're attacking people everywhere, and the ones who don't die turn into them. Yep, they turn and, like, fast. It's a horror movie come to life!" Paul said frantically.

Shocked by Paul's rambling, Kevin said, "Have a seat. Can I get you a glass of water?"

"Kevin, where's Meg?" Paul asked.

Megan appeared in the hallway. "I'm here, Paul. What's wrong?"

"Oh, Meg, you should see it. People are going crazy, people attacking each other, biting them, others turning crazy and then attacking. The world has gone insane!"

"Calm down. What are you talking about?" Megan asked, a look of fear stretched across her face.

Kevin found the television remote and turned it on. The last channel that Megan was watching had been news, and when the picture appeared, it was full of images of chaos and destruction.

Megan walked towards the television to get a better look, her hand covering her mouth. "Oh my God, Kev, this is what I was talking about last night, but it's gotten worse."

"It's the end of the world," Paul bellowed.

"Don't say that, Paul," Kevin warned.

Gunshots sounded just outside their apartment building.

"What was that? Was that someone shooting?" Megan exclaimed.

"Guys, that's what I've been saying—the world is

ending. The shit is hitting the fan right fucking now!" Paul yelled.

Megan turned to Kevin and asked, "What should we do?"

"Ah, they normally recommend to shelter in place..." Kevin said but stopped when he heard the newscaster repeat the exact words he said. "See, they said shelter in place."

"But I thought you didn't trust the news," Megan said.

"I don't, but...shit, let me think," Kevin said, his eyes glued to the grisly scenes playing out on the screen.

Another series of gunshots sounded outside, this time closer.

Kevin ran to the window and looked down from his fifth-story perch. On the street below, people were racing around, frantic. In the distance he heard more gunfire, sirens, and saw several smoke plumes rising high into the sky.

Megan came up behind him and looked out. "Dear God, it is the end of the world."

"Told you," Paul said.

"We have to leave," Megan said.

Kevin looked at her, nodded and said, "You know something, I agree. Go grab clothes for us. I'll grab some other items we'll need." Kevin took off for a closet in the second bedroom while Megan went to the bedroom.

Megan appeared in the living room with two suitcases.

Kevin emerged from the second bedroom, a shotgun

in one hand and a Glock 17 tucked in his waistband. On his back, a large pack was strapped; in it he had a tent, two sleeping bags, and other camping necessities.

Megan gave him a shocked look and barked, "Guns? You've had guns in the apartment?" Her attention focused on the firearms, she didn't see the enormous backpack.

"Yeah," he answered nonchalantly, going past her and into the kitchen. He placed the shotgun on the counter, removed the pack, and took a trash bag from underneath the counter. He began to fill it with canned food from the pantry. He gave Paul a look, tossed him a spare bag, and said, "Start packing the dry goods and canned food."

Megan stepped in behind them and kept questioning him. "You had guns and never told me?"

Not turning to look at her, he simply replied, "Yes."

"Someone could have gotten hurt," she said.

"Who? I had them locked in that wall locker," Kevin said.

"Well, someone could have," Megan snapped.

Gunshots sounded from outside the building again.

He looked back and said, "You hear that? Don't you think it's a good idea we have some weapons to defend ourselves?"

"That's not the point," she blared.

Annoyed with her questions, he tossed a bag at her and said, "How about helping us instead of talking."

Her face turned flush, but she kept her mouth closed, took the bag, and began to load up essential items in the kitchen.

After packing, they had two suitcases and five large bags of food, as well as Kevin's firearms and a backpack with extra ammunition.

Megan was positioned at the window. She was still in shock at the utter chaos still unfolding on the streets below.

"It's time to go!" Kevin cried.

"Where are we going?" Paul asked. He was standing next to the front door, both arms holding bags of food.

"North out of town, we can head to Bear Lake maybe," Kevin said. Bear Lake was a large natural freshwater lake. It was over one hundred and nine square miles and equally spanned land in northern Utah and southern Idaho.

"I've never been to Bear Lake. I hear it's nice," Paul said.

"There's always a first," Kevin quipped. He gave Megan a glance and said, "Meg, it's time to go."

Still glued to the window, Megan was having a hard time looking away from the violence exploding on the street.

"Meg, time to go!" Kevin hollered.

Megan snapped out of her trance, turned and said, "Let's go before it gets worse."

The trio raced down the stairs, opting to avoid elevators for safety reasons. Their destination was the parking garage below.

They stepped onto the garage level only to run into a bloody and panicked man running towards them.

Kevin dropped what he was carrying, pulled the pistol from his trousers, and raised it at the man. "Don't come close to us or I'll shoot."

The man, who was wild eyed and clearly fleeing something, cried out, "Please help me!"

"Get away," Kevin warned.

The man stopped, held his hands high and said, "Please help me. It's coming, it attacked me, and I managed to get away, please."

"We're trying to get to my girlfriend's truck. Step to the side," Kevin barked.

"Please help me," the man begged.

The heavy pitter-patter of feet echoed off the garage walls.

Kevin looked but didn't see what it was until the very last second.

Out of the shadows a man appeared. He leapt at the other and took him to the ground. Within seconds he began to bite and claw at the helpless man who had been pleading for help.

The three recoiled from the sight.

Megan started to run back up the stairs, fearful that soon they'd be a target.

Paul stood frozen in shock and terror.

Kevin, on the other hand, knew the only way to get out of town was in Megan's truck, and the only thing in his way was the person savagely attacking the man. He advanced, gun cradled in both hands, took aim on the attacker, and squeezed the trigger. The nine-millimeter round struck the attacker in the shoulder.

It looked up, blood covering its body and face. It snarled at him and stood up as if it hadn't even been shot.

Kevin was in shock.

"Shoot him!" Megan screamed from the stairwell.

Paul still remained fixed to his spot.

Kevin squeezed off several more rounds, each striking it in the upper torso.

It took a single step before its knees buckled and it fell to the floor dead.

"Hurry, I think he's dead," Kevin shouted, his hand shaking. He'd never shot anyone before, much less killed anyone.

Megan took the cue and sprinted back down the stairs. She grabbed Paul's arm and dragged him along. They reached Kevin, who had walked over to the first man, who was still alive but badly injured from the attack.

"Help," the man said, his voice weak.

"We need to help him," Megan said.

"And do what with him?" Kevin asked.

"Drop him at a hospital," Megan snapped.

"I think we need to keep moving, get out of town," Kevin said, his thoughts coming purely from self-preservation. Any additional stops could jeopardize their ability to get to a safe place.

"Are you crazy? The man is in need of help. What kind of person walks away from someone in need?" Megan scolded.

As the two bickered, Paul watched as the man gasped his last breath, and said, "Hey, guys."

Megan and Kevin didn't hear Paul above their back-

and-forth.

Speaking louder, Paul said, "Hey, guys!"

Kevin looked at Paul and asked, "What?"

"He's dead. The guy is dead," Paul said, pointing at the man, who lay with his eyes wide open.

"Problem solved," Kevin said. "Come on, we need to go." He took off running towards the truck, with Paul and Megan close behind.

They reached the truck without further incident and got in.

After Megan closed her door and put on her seatbelt, she gave Kevin a sour look and said, "When we get to wherever we're going, you and I need to have a talk."

Ignoring her, Kevin started the truck, put it into gear, and slammed his foot against the accelerator. The truck's rear tires spun on the slick concrete floor of the garage before gripping and lurching forward. Kevin turned the wheel hard to the right; up ahead was the exit.

A man covered in blood jumped out in front of them. He had the same deranged look on his face.

"Kevin, watch out!" Megan screamed, pointing at the man as if Kevin didn't see him.

Narrowing his eyes and clenching his jaw, Kevin applied more pressure to the gas.

"Watch out!" Megan cried, not expecting that he'd try to hit the man.

The man bounced off the grille of the truck and hit the ground just in front of them. Kevin kept the gas pedal down and ran over him.

"Oh my God, you...you ran him over!" Megan

shouted in disbelief.

"What would you rather I do, give him a lift?" Kevin countered.

They exited the parking structure and onto the side street. Now they had a full view of the chaos erupting.

Kevin turned the steering wheel hard to the left. The truck strained under the maneuver and tossed Megan and Paul against the right-side door.

"Hold on!" Kevin hollered.

"Don't kill us trying to save us," Megan snarked.

Kevin quickly navigated a few side streets until he had gotten them to the on-ramp for Interstate 15. He prayed the freeway wasn't busy as he sped up the on-ramp. When he had a full view of the six lanes heading north, he sighed in relief, as his prayers were answered.

The interstate had minimal traffic. It was expected, as it was a Sunday, but after waking to the events this morning, he could have also imagined a clogged freeway with everyone trying to do what he was doing.

A surge of joy ran through him as he felt they had escaped what could have been a tragic day for them. He reached over and touched Megan's hand and asked, "Are you okay?"

She smiled and said, "No, I'm not. I don't know what's going on, but we should find out."

"Turn on the radio," Paul suggested, leaning over the front bench seat.

"Good idea," Megan said, hitting the power button on the radio. She then gave Kevin a look and said, "And good idea on having a gun, I change my opinion on that matter."

Kevin gave her a quick glance and quipped, "See, sometimes I'm right."

She tuned to the FM dial and quickly found an announcement. *"The following message is being transmitted by the Emergency Broadcast System. By order of the Department of Homeland Security and all state and local authorities, all individuals living in the United States should seek shelter and wait for further instructions. If you are outside, it is advised to promptly find shelter. This is not a test. This is an actual national emergency. Repeat, by order of the Department of Homeland Security and all state and local authorities…"*

Megan turned the channel with hopes of finding a live broadcast that could help tell them what was happening. She tuned to a local rock station and found a disc jockey talking.

"…sure how long I'll be on the air, as the general manager has told us to evacuate to our homes or shelters, but to anyone listening out there—go find someplace safe, get off the streets. I had callers trying to reach us, but now the phone lines are so jammed they're down. People, please listen, go find someplace safe. I don't know what the hell is going on, but people are going fucking crazy. Yes, I just cursed and I'll take the fine. Listen, I don't think this is some zombie apocalypse, as some have said. The people that are attacking others aren't dead, they're very much alive and can be killed like anyone else. I don't know if they're hopped up on drugs or there's some sort of brainwashing. Right now your biggest concern should be finding a place to go and get off the streets."

"I told you things were getting bad," Megan said, reminding Kevin of her concerns last night.

"You were right, I'm sorry," Kevin said.

Megan turned around and began talking to Paul while Kevin kept his focus on the road. As his heart rate began to come down, he went through the events of the past hour. It was hard to believe that so much had transpired so quickly. He wasn't sure if his life was forever changed or this was a mere blip and everything would get back under control. He had confidence in law enforcement and the military to handle this, but at the same time a tiny bit of fear resided in him that what he'd just encountered could be his new normal.

"Your hand is shaking," Megan said to Kevin.

Snapping out of his deep thoughts, he asked, "Who, me?"

"Yeah, you're shaking. Must have been the trauma. I'm sure we'll all have PTSD from what just happened."

"I already have it," Paul quipped.

Kevin looked into the rearview mirror and snarled, "Let's not make fun of that."

"I was only joking," Paul said.

"Don't be so harsh on him," Megan said, defending her little brother.

"I'm not being harsh, and we all very well might end up with some post-traumatic issues. I just don't like when people make jokes about it, that's all," Kevin said.

"Fair enough," Megan said, an inquisitive eye focused on Kevin's left hand shaking. "What now?"

"We drive to Bear Lake and camp out for a while. See if this dies down," Kevin said.

"What about your parents?" Megan asked.

"I forgot about them; I'm a horrible son. Can you call them?" Kevin asked Megan.

"Shit, I forgot my phone," she said, tapping all her pockets.

"I have mine. What's the number?" Paul asked. "But I doubt it will work. I tried calling you guys this morning; then the phones stopped working. Said all circuits are busy."

Kevin gave him the number.

Paul dialed the number and said, "Same message as earlier, all circuits are busy. Says we should try the call again later."

"Guys, I don't know what the hell is going on or for how long it will happen. What I do know is if we're going to make it, we need to stick together. We're a team now. We need to think differently, act differently. However we viewed the world yesterday is gone for now. I love you both and want us to make it out of this in one piece," Kevin said.

"I agree," Megan said.

"You love me, bro?" Paul joked.

"Sometimes I wonder why, but yeah, I love you." Kevin laughed.

"We're family; we stick together," Megan said, reaching back over her seat and touching Paul's hand.

"Love you, sis," Paul said.

Kevin passed a sign that read *BEAR LAKE STATE PARK 117 MILES*. "I suggest everyone get some rest. We don't know what the day will look like."

"What about you?" Megan asked.

"I can do one hundred and seventeen miles easily; plus I want to think about what our next step should be."

"I thought it was to camp out and wait for this to die down?" Megan asked.

He glanced at her and said soberly, "But what if it doesn't die down?"

CHAPTER FOUR

BIG BEAR LAKE, UTAH

JUNE 1, 2020

Kevin woke early to see if any new information could be heard. He jumped in the truck and grabbed his phone, which he'd left on the charger. Glancing at the screen, he found it still had no service, leaving him only the radio. He turned the power on; the truck's dash lights came to life and flashed. That was when he noticed they were low on fuel. The radio was on but the volume down. He flipped through station after station but only found the Emergency Broadcast System's message they had heard yesterday. He flipped to the AM dial and discovered the same thing. *How is that possible?* he thought.

"Anything?" Megan asked, suddenly appearing at the driver's side door.

Startled, he jumped and said, "God, you scared me."

"You're jumpy." She laughed.

"Who wouldn't be?" he replied.

"My back hurts; that ground was so hard," she complained, shrugging her shoulders and stretching.

Kevin looked past her and asked, "Where's Paul?"

"Still sleeping," she answered.

"Listen, we're really low on gas. I need to go find some. I'm going to go look around for a map to see where a station might be," he said.

"Just use your phone," she said instinctually.

"No service, totally worthless," he said, holding up his smartphone. "Technology is great when it works, but when it doesn't, we have to go back to the good old ways of doing things."

"Where will you find a map?" Megan asked.

"Again the old-fashioned way, first I'll ask around; then I'll go to the ranger station and see if there are any there," Kevin said. "Say, I want Paul to come with me. He could use the walk."

Megan put her hands on her hips and snarled at Kevin, "Don't make fun of his weight."

"I'm just saying he could do with shedding more than a few pounds. A walk will do him some good," Kevin countered. "And I'm not making fun. If we're going to survive, we need to look after each other and be able to carry our own pack, as they say."

"Oh, we're in the army now?" Megan quipped.

Kevin stepped out of the truck, closed the door, and locked it. "No, I'm merely saying that he needs to be physically ready. What if the truck breaks down and we have to walk somewhere?"

"That's not going to happen," Megan snapped, fully knowing her comment was silly and unrealistic.

"That won't happen, but a bunch of people running around savagely killing people is totally possible?" Kevin said. "You know, Meg, you defend him too much; in fact, you coddle him."

"I do not," she said.

Kevin headed to the camp to wake Paul up. Megan

was close behind.

"He needs support is all," Megan said.

Kevin reached the campsite and tapped Paul on the butt with his foot. "Wake up, sunshine, time to get up."

Paul rolled over, yawned and said, "Oh, hi, good morning." He tossed off a blanket to reveal five protein bar wrappers and an empty bag of potato chips.

Kevin shook his head and barked, "You ate all that!"

Paul looked around at the wrappers and said, "I was hungry."

"We only have so much food, Paul. We need to ration it," Kevin said, glaring at Paul.

"I'm sorry, Kevin, don't be mad," Paul whimpered.

"We'll find more food," Megan said.

"Jesus Christ, Meg, we don't know what we're going to find. We don't know shit. C'mon now, stop defending him even when you know he's clearly made a mistake. Paul, you can't just free feed," Kevin roared.

"Stop yelling," Megan said, picking up the wrappers.

"You baby him, Meg. This is stupid," Kevin snapped.

"Well, maybe he needs some tender loving care," Megan said.

"He's twenty-four; last time I checked, that's a man," Kevin shot back.

"His parents died when he was little, he didn't have a real childhood, and he's…" she said then looked at Paul, who was still sitting on the ground moping. "He's different."

Annoyed to the point of losing his cool and saying

something he might regret, Kevin turned and walked off. "I'll be back shortly and, Paul, try not to eat all our food."

"Screw you, Kevin," Megan yelled back.

Kevin ignored her and strutted away.

***

After hiking down the gravel road they used to enter the park, Kevin found the ranger station. As he expected, it was empty. He tried the door to find it unlocked. He opened it and went inside. The building was small. Plastered on the far wall was exactly what he was looking for, a map of the park and general area. He headed right for it, found his location, then discovered something better than a gas station; he found the location of the park maintenance area. As a teenager he'd worked at a state park, and he recalled that the park's maintenance area had gasoline pumps; he just hoped the power was still on there. He scoured the station for food and water, but found only a melted chocolate bar in a desk and a half-full bottle of water. He took both; his thinking was they could come in handy if food became scarce.

He turned to leave and saw a woman standing in the doorway.

"Do you work here?" she asked.

"Ah, no," he replied.

"I haven't seen a ranger for days," she said. Her long dark hair was pulled back into a ponytail, and her skin had an olive complexion. She was wearing a tank top and shorts; she was easily able to pull off that look because her body was toned and fit.

Kevin was instantly attracted to her but pushed his primal desires aside. "How long have you been here?"

"Four days, I'm out here with friends from college for an end-of-school camping trip," she said.

He approached her with his hand extended. "My name is Kevin."

She took a step back out of caution. Not taking his hand, she said, "Sabrina."

Kevin looked at his dangling hand and pulled it back. "I won't hurt you. I'm here with my girlfriend and her brother. We just arrived yesterday."

"Do you know what's going on?" she asked.

"No, but I know it's bad. People for some reason are attacking other people, killing them. It's gotten so bad they've evacuated some major cities. We live in SLC and had to leave; the chaos was getting pretty bad," Kevin said.

"I'm from back east. I spoke to my parents three days ago. They were going to a shelter. I haven't heard from them since," Sabrina said.

"Where was this?" Kevin asked.

"Maryland, just outside DC," Sabrina answered.

The two stood speechless for a second before Kevin spoke up. "I'm going to head back to my campsite. If you and your friends are looking for company, we're at campsite thirty-three."

"We might do that. Do you have any booze?" she asked.

"No, we don't," Kevin replied.

"We do. If you have any spare food, we're up for exchanging a bottle for something to eat," she said.

Kevin thought for a minute and said, "Come by later. I need to see how much we have."

She stepped away from the door, making enough space for Kevin to exit.

He exited the ranger station, gave her a nod and said, "Hope to see you and your friends later."

She smiled and walked off.

Kevin watched her leave for more than a few seconds before scolding himself for flirting. "What's wrong with you?"

***

Back at the campsite, Kevin went directly to the truck. He was still annoyed with both Megan and Paul, and the last thing he needed was Megan chastising him some more.

He turned on the truck, put it into gear, and started to back out.

Megan ran up and smacked the hood. "Hold on!"

Kevin stopped and rolled down the window. "Yeah?"

"You come back but don't say anything?" Megan said, walking up to his window.

"I don't have time. I think I might have found a place to get gas," he said bluntly.

"Can Paul come?" she asked.

"Does Paul want to come, or do you want him to come?" Kevin asked.

Paul ran up and gave Kevin his answer. "Hey, Kev, can I join you?"

Kevin gripped the steering wheel tight. Having to spend time at this very moment with Paul wasn't something he wanted to do.

"Well, can he?" Megan asked.

"Hop in," Kevin said, unlocking the passenger door.

"Take care of him," Megan said.

Kevin rolled his eyes, then put up the window.

Paul jumped in and buckled up. "Where are we going?"

"To the maintenance area," Kevin said and sped off down the gravel road, leaving Megan in a cloud of dust.

After a couple of miles and a few turns, they arrived at a locked gate.

"It's locked," Paul said, seeing a large padlock on the bottom of a fork latch.

"I see that. Maybe we can find a hacksaw or bolt cutters somewhere," Kevin said with a look of frustration on his face.

Paul opened the door and hopped out.

"Where are you going?" Kevin asked.

"To unlock it," Paul said, keeping the door open.

"With what?" Kevin asked.

Paul walked up to the gate, removed his wallet, fished around and pulled out what looked to Kevin to be two small sticks. He knelt in front of the lock and inserted one, then another. Seconds later the lock popped open. He removed the padlock, tossed it aside, opened the fork latch, and shoved the gates open enough for the truck to pass through.

A broad smile creased across Kevin's face. "Well, what do you know?" He drove through the gate and stopped.

Paul got back in, a huge smile on his face as well.

"You know how to pick locks?" Kevin asked.

"I know a few more things too," Paul said proudly.

"Huh," Kevin said before driving into the maintenance area.

They found a gasoline pump, and fortunately the power was still on.

As Kevin filled the truck, Paul went looking for spare gas cans. He found some in one of the bays along with a large toolbox. He tossed it in the back of the truck. "Thought we could use this."

"Smart, anything else?" Kevin asked.

"I'll go look around," Paul said and headed back inside the maintenance bays. He returned with two large bags. He lowered the tailgate and placed them on it.

Kevin finished topping off the gas cans and put them in the bed. "What do you have there?"

Paul slowly emptied the bags. "Some food—crackers, chips and cookies. And I found a refrigerator and got some Gatorade, bottled water and an energy drink," he said with a smile. "Hopefully this will make up for my gluttony last night."

Kevin peeked inside the bag and asked, "What else you got in there?"

"Overalls, fireproof, might come in handy. A roll of plastic sheeting, work gloves, engine oil, radiator fluid, brake fluid, an assortment of batteries, two flashlights, rope, a lighter, pens, notebook; with our phones dead, we might need to write things down."

"You got a lot of good stuff," Kevin said happily.

"That's not all," Paul said, reaching into the second bag. "Two cans of Fix-A-Flat, duct tape, three face ventilators, four pairs of goggles, some rubber bands, a first aid kit, saline solution, and the grand finale, a Slim Jim. Dude, we can open locked cars easily now."

"Nice job," Kevin said. He spotted something else in the bag. "What's that?"

"Nothing." Paul blushed, trying to close the bag before Kevin reached in and grabbed it.

"A *Hustler* magazine? I didn't know they published these anymore with all the free online porn," Kevin said, flipping through it casually.

Paul snatched it from Kevin and said, "Don't tell Meg."

"I won't, you dirty dog," Kevin said, winking. "I'm seriously proud of you, what a mother lode. You did a damn good job today."

"Thanks," Paul said, lowering his head shyly.

"Come on, let's get back and celebrate with Megan," Kevin said.

"Hey, Kev," Paul said.

Stopping, Kevin asked, "What is it?"

"My sister means well, but I don't need to be treated like a child. She feels sorry for me, and I admit I let her do it sometimes. I know that I can't continue to do things the way I used to. I know I need to be better, stronger and help out. I don't want you to cut me slack just 'cause she says so."

"I won't, but you need to tell her that, not me," Kevin said.

"I've tried," Paul lamented.

"Then try again. Tonight, tell her in front of me; I'll defend you."

"You will?" Paul asked.

"Of course. I think of you as a brother, and right now I need you just as much as you need me. Like I said yesterday, we need to be a team if we're going to survive this."

"I agree," Paul said.

"How about we get to the campsite and show Megan everything you got us today?" Kevin said.

"Good idea," Paul said, slamming the tailgate.

***

The trio spent the remaining part of the day and early evening sorting through the loot Paul had found and stashing it in the truck.

Megan was proud of Paul but even happier that Kevin had allowed him to contribute.

"Now that that's done, I think we should talk about setting up a night watch," Kevin said, taking a seat in front of the fire.

"You think we need it?" Megan asked.

"I agree with Kev, and I'll volunteer for the first shift," Paul said.

Megan gave him an odd look and asked, "You do?"

"Yeah, it's smart. We have a truck, fuel and now a lot of gear; we need to keep watch over it," Paul said.

Kevin smiled and said, "Everything he said, but the shifts should be three hours starting at ten. We will rotate who starts the shift to be fair," Kevin said.

"Since you two think it's a good idea and I can't find a reason to oppose it, I agree," Megan said.

"Knock, knock," a woman said from the shadows.

The trio turned towards the voice.

"Who's that?" Kevin asked.

Sabrina stepped into the light. "It's Sabrina. We met earlier."

"Oh yes, hi," Kevin said, standing up. He turned to Megan and said, "This is Sabrina. I met her at the ranger station earlier."

Sabrina was followed by two other people, a man and a woman. "This is Trent and Ashley."

Kevin, Megan and Paul all greeted them and welcomed them to take a seat around the fire.

"I have a bottle of Fireball to trade," she said, pulling it out of a bag. "What do you have?"

"Oh, um," he said to Sabrina. He faced Megan and said, "I said we might be up for a trade of food for a bottle of booze."

"You did, huh?" Megan said, her lip curled in a way that showed Kevin she was not amused.

"Paul, you want some Fireball?" Kevin asked.

"I've never had it," Paul said, his gaze fixed on Ashley.

Ashley was short, standing about five feet two, and had long blond hair, large breasts and milky skin. By all accounts she was considered attractive.

"For some food you can have it," Sabrina said.

"Can I try it first?" Paul asked.

Sabrina looked at Ashley and Trent, who nodded their approval. She opened the bottle, handed it to Paul, and said, "One drink, no more."

Paul hesitated at first, unsure what to expect.

"It tastes like spicy cinnamon," Megan said.

Paul put the bottle to his lips, tipped it back and took a gulp. After he swallowed, he started to cough.

Sabrina laughed. "You don't drink much, do you?"

Handing the bottle back to Sabrina, Paul said, "Not really."

"No deal," Megan snapped.

"But we were under the impression you'd like to make a deal," Sabrina said.

"Well, we're not," Megan fired back.

Seeing the tension build, Kevin stepped in, "Do you have any vodka?"

Sabrina looked at Trent and Ashley. Trent gave her a nod.

"We have a bottle of Ketel One," Sabrina said.

"What do you want for that?" Kevin asked.

"We're not trading food for alcohol," Megan snapped.

Ignoring Megan, Sabrina put her attention on Kevin and said, "Enough food that will last us a day, three meals."

"Three meals for the three of you? No," Kevin said.

Sabrina once more looked at her friends.

"Enough for two meals and three bottles of water," Trent said.

"Here's what you'll get, three cans of baked beans, three cans of corn, nothing else. Take it or leave it," Kevin said.

"Kevin, what are you doing?" Megan asked.

"Deal," Sabrina blurted out.

"Damn it, Kevin," Megan barked.

"Megan, we can use the alcohol for antiseptic too; plus I could use a drink after everything we've been through," Kevin said.

Sabrina reached into her bag and pulled out the bottle of Ketel. She walked across the campsite and handed it to Kevin. "Here you go. Where's the food?"

"Come with me," Kevin said.

The two walked to Kevin's tent. He pulled a bag from inside and pulled out the desired cans, handing them to her.

She held them up and said, "Good deal, thank you."

"Thank you," Kevin said.

"Your girlfriend, she's bossy," Sabrina said.

"She has an opinion, like all of us," Kevin said.

"Do you mind if we eat here with you all? It's sort of nice meeting new people considering everything that's going on," she said.

"Sure," Kevin said, knowing that Megan would protest, but at the moment he didn't care.

The two went back to the fire.

Sabrina divided the cans between her and her friends, who immediately opened them up and began to devour the beans and corn.

Kevin sat back down and watched.

Megan glared at Kevin, her jaw clenched and arms crossed.

Wanting to spark up a conversation, Kevin asked, "Have you seen any of the attacks yet?"

"Just a few videos on our phones when they worked," Trent replied. "Have you?"

"Yes," Kevin said.

"Kev killed one," Paul said proudly.

"You did?" Sabrina asked, looking up from her can of beans.

"I had to do it; it was attacking someone," Kevin said.

"You both have referred to the people attacking as if they're not human," Sabrina said, noticing the terms *it* and *one*.

"They look human, I suppose; though did you notice the huge black pupils of that one you killed?" Paul asked.

"I didn't. I think I had tunnel vision. All I saw was a man covered in blood, biting and ripping at another man," Kevin said.

"Do you think they're all on drugs like that one, what was it?" Ashley asked.

"Flakka," Sabrina replied.

"Yeah, that one," Ashley said.

"Maybe it's bath salts," Trent said.

"I don't think that's what it is. It's like these people

aren't people; it's like they're animals, like they're mutated," Kevin said.

"It's a mutant apocalypse," Paul said with a smile.

"You think this is funny?" Sabrina asked.

"Ah, no, just coining a phrase," Paul said.

"Yeah, a mutant apocalypse, that's kinda like a zombie apocalypse," Trent said.

"Except mutants are alive…" Paul said.

"And zombies are dead," Trent said, completing his thought.

"Exactly!" Paul yelped.

"Now that we've established that these two are apocalypse fan boys, what do you all have planned?" Sabrina asked.

"To hang out and see what happens, I suppose," Kevin answered.

"We're thinking about heading to Twin Falls. I have some family there," Sabrina said.

Unable to handle any more small talk and beyond annoyed, Megan blurted, "It's almost ten, time for us to go to bed and start our watch."

Sabrina raised her brow and said, "You all have a bedtime?"

"No, we just set up a time for a night watch, and it begins at ten," Kevin said, trying to make what Megan said not sound immature.

"We sort of do have a bedtime, meaning whoever has other shifts should get to bed so they're rested, right, Kevin?" Megan growled then gave Kevin a hard stare.

"I see that we've worn out our welcome. Thank you

for the trade, and maybe we'll see you around the park," Sabrina said, standing up.

Trent and Ashley followed her lead.

"Have a good night," Kevin said.

"You too," Sabrina said. The three walked off into the darkness.

Megan walked up to Kevin and pelted him on the arm. "I saw how you were looking at her."

"Who?" Kevin asked.

"Sabrina. I saw you!" Megan exclaimed, waving her finger.

"I don't know what you're talking about," Kevin said, walking off towards his tent.

"Don't think about cuddling up to me later," Megan fired back.

"Go easy on him," Paul said.

"You're on his side?" Megan asked.

"He's a good guy, and you can be a bit judgmental."

"I'm your sister and I'm not judgmental. If I didn't look out for everyone—"

"None of us need a mother, Meg. I appreciate you thinking you're mine, but you're not. The world has changed, and I'm going to change with it," Paul said confidently.

Kevin was in the shadows, overhearing the conversation. He was happy Paul was sticking up for himself and keeping his promise that he'd talk to Megan.

"I'm not acting like your mother," Megan said, defending herself.

"Meg, I love you, I really do, but ease up a bit. I'll be

fine, and Kev is a good guy. I didn't see him looking at Sabrina," Paul said.

"'Cause you were ogling Ashley. Don't think I didn't see you salivating over there," she said.

"I was, so what? She's hot; there, I admit it. Am I not supposed to look at hot chicks, ever?" Paul asked.

"I didn't say that," Megan said.

"Then what were you saying?"

Frustrated by everyone and everything, Megan stormed off.

"Meg, don't go away angry. We can talk about this," Paul called out to her.

Megan ignored his pleas and strode out of the campsite and down the moonlit road.

Kevin emerged from the shadows. "I should go after her."

"You were listening to us?" Paul asked.

"I overheard a little. It wasn't on purpose; the campsite is small," Kevin said.

"No, don't go after her. She needs a little time to decompress," Paul said.

"Are you sure? What if one of those people attacks her?" Kevin asked.

"A feral? I think if one was around here, we'd have heard it by now. Those things are vicious," Paul said.

"You sure?" Kevin asked again.

"Positive, now go to bed. I've got the first shift," Paul said.

"Good job today, and I'll see you in four hours," Kevin said. He turned and went to his tent.

CHAPTER FIVE

BIG BEAR LAKE, UTAH

JUNE 2, 2020

"Kevin, wake up!" Paul shouted.

Kevin opened his eyes, but all he saw around him was darkness. He sat up but could tell Megan wasn't there. In the distance was the sound of heavy gunfire as if a battle was under way.

"Kevin, get up. Something is going on, and Megan never came back!" Paul hollered, panic in his voice.

Hearing that Megan hadn't returned sent a shiver down Kevin's spine. "How long has she been gone?" Kevin asked as he put on his shoes.

"Since you went to bed," Paul replied.

"When was that? I don't know what time it is," Kevin said, grabbing his Glock and unzipping the tent. He stepped out into the crisp night air.

Paul stood feet from him, a flashlight in his hand.

The gunfire kept going, volley after volley of automatic and heavy machine-gun fire.

"Sounds like a war out there," Paul said.

"Stay here; watch our stuff. I'm going to go find Meg," Kevin said and took off at a full sprint towards the truck.

A beam from another flashlight crossed his path.

"Who's that?" Kevin called out. "Meg, is that you?"

"No, it's Sabrina. I heard the gunfire and didn't know what was going on. I thought…I don't know what I thought. Is your girlfriend gone?" Sabrina asked.

"Yeah, we…" Kevin said, about to disclose their fight but stopped short of doing so. "She went for a walk and has been gone for two hours now."

"She took a midnight stroll?" Sabrina asked.

"I can't talk right now," Kevin said, unlocking the truck and getting in.

"Can we help?" Sabrina asked.

"You know something, you can. Can you drive south and look for her?" Kevin asked.

"Yeah, we can do that," Sabrina said and immediately took off towards her camp.

Kevin sped off north down the gravel drive that led to the interstate. With the window rolled down, he called out, "Megan! Megan!" He knew he was drawing attention to himself, but at the moment he didn't care.

Miles and miles he drove, but nothing; it was as if she had disappeared. He noticed the gunfire had ceased. Had she been somehow involved in that? he wondered. But how? It was another mile or two away by the sound of it. There was no way she could have made it, nor would she have walked that far.

Around and around he drove through the park calling her name. The minutes turned to hours, and still he hadn't found her.

He returned to camp to see if she had shown up, but she hadn't. His concern was now turning to gut-wrenching panic.

"Kev, is she dead, huh, do you think she's dead?" Paul asked, his voice cracking.

"We don't know anything. She's probably lost is all," Kevin said, attempting to ease his fears though he was close to needing to be reassured too.

Headlights of a car approached.

Kevin touched the back strap of his Glock tucked in his waistband and waited to see who it was.

The driver's door opened and out stepped Sabrina. "Kevin, you need to come with me."

Hearing those words and the tone she used told him everything. "Where is she?"

"Oh no, no," Paul wailed, tears flowing from his eyes, as he too knew what Sabrina's tone and word choice meant.

"Just come with me," Sabrina said.

Kevin's legs felt weak. If he took a step, he might crumple to the ground.

Seeing the pain he was in, Sabrina came to him and put her arm around him.

"Where is she?" he asked, his voice trembling with grief.

"She's alive…" Sabrina said.

"Wait, she's alive?" Kevin said, his voice perking up.

"I need you to come with me," Sabrina said.

"What is it?" Kevin asked.

"Oh no, God no." Paul kept crying. He dropped to his knees and was wailing.

"Please, just come. You have to hurry. I don't think she has much time," Sabrina said, finally giving him a clue.

"She's...um...she's been hurt?" Kevin asked.

Taking him by the arm, Sabrina walked Kevin to her car and put him in. In the back Ashley sat, her face showing the intensity and emotion of the situation.

Kevin sat unable to think clearly.

Sabrina got in the car. She touched Kevin's arm and said, "She's asking for you."

Kevin wiped tears from his face and said, "Take me to her."

Sabrina drove a little over a mile down the road south. She pulled off near a fork in the road and got out. She ran over to Kevin's side, but he was out and looking around. "Where is she?"

Trent waved a flashlight. "Over here."

Kevin ran towards Trent. As he got close, he saw the grisly scene feet from where she lay. He slowed his pace and looked around at the blood and bits of her that were strewn everywhere. He glanced up next to Trent and saw Megan's blood-splattered face. To the right of her, he spotted someone else; he looked more closely and saw it was a child.

"Kev...come," Megan said just above a whisper.

He snapped back and went to her side. Taking her hand, he held it close to his chest. "What happened?"

"I went and got myself killed is what I did," she joked.

"No, we'll get you fixed up. Yep, we'll do that," he said, looking at her battered body. Her left arm was shattered, and when he saw her lower abdomen was ripped open, exposing her intestines, his hope vanished. "That child did this to you?"

"I thought she was lost. I was going to help her and she...it attacked me. She was so strong. I managed to get my knife out and stab..." she said but paused as she began to cough. She opened her mouth to talk again, and blood poured out. "I feel strange."

"You're hurt, that's what it is," Kevin said.

"No, I feel strange. I'm having weird sensations. I think...I think I'm turning into one of them," she said.

"No, God no, that's not it. You're in shock is all," Kevin said.

"Where's Paul?" she asked.

"Back at the campsite."

"Good, I wouldn't want him to see me this way," she said. "Kev, remember that promise?"

"Yes."

"I need you to keep that promise. I need you to look after Paul. He'll need you even more with me gone. I know he's trying to be more responsible, but with me gone, he'll be affected; he'll need your strength. Promise me you'll never leave his side."

Tears flowed down Kevin's face and dripped from his chin. "I promise."

"I'm getting cold now, I think..." she said, closing her eyes for a few seconds then opening them. "I'm going to go now."

"Don't leave me," Kevin cried.

"I love you," she said.

"I love you too," he said.

She let out a heavy sigh and closed her eyes.

He waited for her to open her eyes again, but she didn't. "Meg? Meg?"

Sabrina came up behind him and touched his shoulder. "I'm very sorry."

"I, ah, I can't believe she's gone," he said, holding her hand firmly. "What's fucking happening?" he asked, looking at Sabrina before sobbing heavily.

CHAPTER SIX

BIG BEAR LAKE, UTAH

JUNE 4, 2020

Paul was inconsolable. He hadn't left his tent except to bury Megan and then promptly returned to it afterwards. Having lost his parents at an early age and now losing his only living relative was bringing back all the pain of his childhood.

Kevin didn't know what to do or how to handle it, but he'd promised and meant to keep his word to Megan.

Sabrina, Trent and Ashley kept stopping by and eventually decided to move their campsite next to theirs so they could help Kevin.

Kevin welcomed their proximity and liked having others around. They hadn't worked out a formal arrangement, but they all seemed to be working well with each other.

After Megan's random attack, they devised a watch list, rotating people twenty-four hours a day. They also came to the conclusion after the child attacked Megan that whatever was changing people could be contagious.

The gunfire from the other night was still unexplained, but Sabrina and Kevin agreed to finally find out what had happened.

Kevin found Sabrina, Trent and Ashley to be interesting, unique and, with Megan gone, a breath of fresh air. With them around all the time, Kevin watched and listened so he could get to know them better, and after two days had come away with a good snapshot of who his new friends were and their idiosyncrasies.

If someone had to describe Trent with one word, it would be *surfer*. If they were given two words, they would no doubt be *surfer dude*. It wasn't just his look, shoulder-length dirty blond hair, which he often whipped off his face with a quick snap of the head, it was his vocabulary—though limited, he always had something to say and it was usually a joke. Trent was very athletic; he'd been a star football player at Stanford until his senior year when he shattered his knee. It was an injury that had ended any chances of becoming a professional, but wasn't enough to stop him from another passion of his, surfing. Although he was a Stanford graduate, along with Ashley and Sabrina, he didn't appear to have learned a thing. He wasn't the most articulate, nor did he seem to have intellectual curiosity.

Ashley, on the other hand, was highly intelligent, yet she was a very quiet person, the polar opposite of Trent. She had graduated with the others and had decided to continue her education at graduate school, seeking a master's in astrophysics. Just the night before she had shared with Kevin intricate details about the star Rigel, which from Earth resides in the constellation Orion. She went on to describe that it's forty thousand times brighter than the Sun and that it radiates blue, her eyes widening like a child's would as she explained it.

And then there was Sabrina, the natural leader of that

group. She had an inner strength and determination that made her tough, but she too was smart. A chemist, she had just secured a job working in a laboratory in San Francisco.

With their pedigree educations, Kevin felt a bit self-conscious at first; he'd spent his first two years at a community college before going to the University of Utah. He'd gotten his degree in marketing and went straight to work for an advertising firm in Salt Lake City. His job had been good, but he wasn't raking in millions. When he'd discussed his past with them, they didn't say a thing, nor did they seem to judge him, making him realize that he was the only one concerned with where he went to school and what he did. *How odd that we're our own toughest critics*, he mused.

"I think I should go," Trent said to Sabrina.

"No, I agree with Kevin; you should stay and watch the campsite while Ashley sleeps," Sabrina said, with Kevin just behind her, loading up the truck.

"Can't Paul keep an eye out?" Trent asked.

"No, he needs more time," Kevin shouted from the truck.

Trent leaned in close to Sabrina and said, "Paul is a pussy. He needs to step up."

"The guy just lost his sister; give him a break," Sabrina said, defending Paul.

"I understand that, but he's incapable of contributing to watch, hell, even getting firewood," Trent said, clearly annoyed by Paul's lack of effort.

"I'll talk with Kevin and sort some things out. I hear

what you're saying, but right now we have a good thing. Kevin is sharing their food; he seems very capable and has weapons, something we didn't have," Sabrina whispered to Trent. She nodded to the shotgun leaning up against the tree.

"I'll stay this one time, but talk to Kevin, sort this out," Trent said before grabbing the shotgun and heading back to the campsite.

Sabrina and Kevin loaded up and began their trek to investigate the gun battle from the other night.

They hadn't gone a mile before Kevin said, "I'll talk to him when I get back."

"Who?" Sabrina asked.

"Paul, I'll talk to him. I agree that he will need to start venturing out. I also need you to understand that I gave my word to Megan to take care of him. If you haven't noticed, he's a bit simple sometimes."

"Can I speak my mind without offending you?" Sabrina asked.

"Sure, go ahead," Kevin answered.

"I think it's an act. I think he's been coddled, and now he's used to doing nothing. He's been programed to act childlike sometimes. He's been rewarded for such behavior by his sister, and now it's how he goes through life."

"I thought you were a chemist?" Kevin quipped.

"My minor was psychology," she said

"Like I said, I'll talk to him. He needs to be part of the team," Kevin said.

"So we're a team now?" Sabrina asked.

He looked at her and said, "Yeah, for right now we are."

"I like that," she flirted.

"At least until we all determine what's next. I know you want to go to Twin Falls; me, I have no idea," Kevin said, seemingly backtracking.

"You can come with us," Sabrina offered.

"That's nice of you, but right now, I don't know where to go," he said.

"What about your parents?" she asked.

"They moved to Florida a couple of years ago—got tired of the Utah winters," Kevin answered.

They came to a fork in the road and slowed.

Kevin leaned over the steering wheel and said, "I think we go left; that leads us out to the freeway, where I think all the shooting came from."

"You're in charge. Let's go," Sabrina said.

They followed the left fork until it intersected at a tee. Left took them to the northbound lanes of the freeway, and right to the southbound lanes.

"Which way?" Kevin asked, looking left.

"Right," Sabrina said.

"Why right?" Kevin asked, his gaze still fixed to the left.

"On account there's bodies and military vehicles all over the place," Sabrina said, pointing.

Kevin snapped his head around and looked. "I think that's it." He turned the steering wheel to the right and accelerated. He slowed as they came upon the first abandoned crashed Humvee and stopped just after it.

"Let's get out and look around."

They both exited the truck, Kevin with his Glock firmly in his hands. Around them lay the carnage of a battle.

"This looks like it sounded the other night," Sabrina said, scanning the site. In total she counted twenty-six bodies, some uniformed soldiers, others in civilian clothes, all laid out around two Humvees and a five-ton truck, which was lying on its side.

"What were they doing here, and how did they get attacked this far out from a major city?" Kevin asked.

"That's why," Sabrina said, pointing to a makeshift sign that read SHELTER/FIELD HOSPITAL.

"Now it makes sense. These are National Guard troops, and they must have been supporting that field hospital."

"Who do you suppose won?" Sabrina asked.

"They did," Kevin said.

"What makes you say that?" Sabrina asked.

"Just a hunch, but I think we should grab what we can use and get out of here," Kevin said, picking up an M16 rifle.

"Should we take one of those?" Sabrina asked, pointing at a Humvee.

"Looks like only one is in good shape," Kevin said, walking to it and opening the driver's door to find the driver still behind the wheel, his throat ripped out. Blood and guts covered the inside. "I think we should pass."

"What's wrong with you? A big old military truck like this can come in handy," Sabrina said, pulling the corpse from the vehicle. His body hit the pavement with a thud.

"Then you're driving it," Kevin said.

"Fine with me," she said, looking inside. "Wait, how do you start this thing?"

Kevin looked over her shoulder and said, "Switch to the left; follow the instructions."

"What's that?" she asked, pointing at the WAIT light above the switch.

"Oh, that makes sense; it's a diesel. You turn the switch to RUN, and that light should turn on. When it turns off, turn the switch all the way to the right, and start it like any other car."

"Were you in the army?" she asked.

"No, grew up in Utah. We know stuff like this," he quipped, giving her a wink.

The two spent the next ten minutes loading up all the weapons, ammunition, MREs, water cans and gas masks they could find. Like the other day, Kevin was feeling better about their situation after discovering all these necessities.

A branch snapped just off the road.

Sabrina was loading the back of the Humvee while Kevin was at his truck doing the same thing. They both looked up and towards the direction of the breaking branch.

Sabrina took an M16 in her hands and pointed it. She didn't know how to use it, but she felt safer with it in her hands.

Pulling his Glock, Kevin stepped away from the truck. He whistled to Sabrina and motioned with his head for her to take cover behind the Humvee.

She did as he said.

He stepped slowly back towards his truck, ready for anything to happen.

Out of the woods came a man wearing civilian clothing. On his back he had a pack, and slung against his chest was an M4 rifle. He looked weary and disheveled.

Kevin raised his pistol and shouted, "Stop right there. Don't take another step."

The man raised his arms and said, "I'm not a feral."

"What's that? Is that one of those crazy people?" Kevin shouted.

"Yes, it's what we call them," the man said, his arms still raised high.

"Who's we?" Kevin asked.

"The United States government, that's who," the man replied.

"How do I know you're not one of those ferals?" Kevin asked, his heart rate elevated and his hands shaking.

"'Cause I haven't attacked you," the man answered.

"Listen, we're just leaving. You stay where you are and let us go," Kevin said, backing up a couple more feet towards his truck.

"Do me a favor and leave some of that food," the man asked.

"Were you part of this convoy?" Sabrina asked, popping her head above the back end of the Humvee.

"No, I'm from Nellis Air Force Base," the man said.

"Where's that?" Sabrina asked.

"Listen, you two, I'm tired, my arms are feeling really heavy right now, and I'm hungry. I don't want to play this back-and-forth question and answer. I'll answer any question you want about what has happened, 'cause I know what happened; I just need to eat. Can we make a deal?" the man asked.

Sabrina and Kevin gave each other a look, with Kevin deciding to make the call. "Fine, but if you try anything, I'll shoot you," Kevin warned.

"I won't try anything. Just let me have one of those MREs," the man said.

Sabrina walked out from behind the Humvee, reached into the back, and took a single MRE from an open case and tossed it into the middle of the road, feet from her.

"I'm going to lower my arms and advance towards you. Please don't shoot me," the man said.

Kevin lowered his pistol but stayed at a safe distance.

The man approached, grabbed the MRE, and walked back towards the crashed Humvee. He sat down next to it and rested his back against the rear right tire. He ripped open the MRE and poured out its contents. He fished around, found the entrée and opened it. After the first spoonful, he sighed heavily and said, "Let me give you some valuable advice. Don't touch a damn thing that has blood on it. That's how it's transferred."

Kevin and Sabrina gave each other a concerned look.

"Wait, you touched some blood recently, didn't you?" the man asked.

"My girlfriend was killed by one of those ferals. We

all touched her body as we buried her," Kevin confessed.

"When was that?" the man asked.

"Over two days ago," Kevin replied.

"Then you're fine. The mutation happens fairly quickly. Some people turn within an hour; others it takes up to six hours. There are no accounts of days; I think you're fine," the man said.

"What's going on? What happened to the government, the military?" Sabrina asked, stepping towards the man.

"You see this convoy? That's what happened. We got ambushed, so to speak. We didn't take the threat seriously, and then when it was too late, shit went sideways. What's left of the government has gone underground. The military and other EMS are in shambles. It's a total shit show, so if you're expecting the government to come riding in to save you, you're mistaken. They've retreated to the safety of their luxury bunkers and plan on waiting this thing out. The rest of us have to fight it out now; my bets are on the ferals. Last estimate is there are tens of millions of them around the world."

"Wait, this is around the world?" Kevin asked.

"Yep, all it took were more than a few people to hop on a plane, and boom, spread like wildfire there too. Yes, there are pockets not affected. Northern Canada, many of the island nations, Australia and New Zealand made out just fine. The other countries acted like we did, didn't take it seriously; then they were overwhelmed."

"What is it?" Sabrina asked.

"You know, I'm not a scientist, but it's some sort of genetic mutation," the man answered.

"How?" Sabrina asked, her chemistry mind kicking in.

"I don't know. I just know it can be passed from one person to another," the man said.

"But how?" she asked, more to herself than him.

"I said I don't know," the man replied.

"What you're telling us is it's over, the government has abandoned us, no one is coming to help?" Kevin asked.

Shoving a spoonful of food into his mouth, the man replied, "Yes."

Disheartened, Kevin sighed.

"Where are you going?" Sabrina asked.

"To the Yukon, I have an old buddy that has a compound of sorts. It's so remote there isn't a feral anywhere. You're more than welcome to join me," the man said.

"Wait, why would you invite us to come with you? You don't even know us," Kevin asked.

"On account you seem like nice people. You gave me some food; other people just shoot and don't even bother to ask a question. I'll admit I was watching you, and you look like you could use some help. I'm handy with a gun, and I have a secure place to go," the man said.

Sabrina gave Kevin a look, unsure what to do, although her instincts were to allow him into their ragtag group.

Kevin walked up to the man, stuck his hand out and

said, "My name is Kevin."

The man wiped his right hand on his trousers and took Kevin's hand. "Nice to meet you, Kevin. I'm Jason."

"That's Sabrina there," Kevin said, nodding towards her.

"Hi," she said.

"I saw you dragging a bloody body out of that Hummer there. I suggest you don't think about taking it," Jason said, getting to his feet.

"But we can clean it up," Sabrina said.

"Remember what my first bit of advice was?" Jason asked, eyeing the inside of the Humvee.

"Don't touch anything that has blood on it," Sabrina recited.

"Exactly. You don't know anything about the guy driving. The best practice is to avoid anything with blood. That's why in the future, no burying people. They lie where they die, straight and simple," Jason said.

Jason's confidence allured Sabrina. She gave him a once-over and liked what she saw.

"But it's a perfectly good Humvee," Kevin said.

"Then you drive it," Jason said, walking to the back and looking inside the open hatch. "Let's load this up in the truck."

Sabrina went to work doing as he said.

"Where are you staying?" Jason asked.

"A campsite at the park," Kevin answered.

"Good, anyone else there?" Jason asked.

"A couple of other families, but we haven't stayed in contact with anyone," Kevin replied.

"How many vehicles?" Jason asked.

"Two, the truck and they have a Subaru Outback," Kevin answered.

"Good, is the truck four-wheel drive?" Jason asked.

"Yeah."

"Great, this is great. And how many others?" Jason asked.

Feeling uneasy that he was giving so much information up, Kevin asked, "How do I know you're not part of a bigger group trying to get info on us?"

"You don't, but I can tell you, if I was part of a bigger group and wanted info, I would've shot you before I came out of those woods, then forced you to give up your friends," Jason said confidently.

"I would've shot you with this," Sabrina said, holding up the M16.

"Show me how to use that," Jason said.

She looked down at it and fumbled with it before he took it out of her hands and pointed at the open chamber. "The bolt is locked back; the weapon is empty." He dropped the magazine and showed her. "You weren't going to do anything with this."

Feeling foolish, Sabrina asked, "Can you show us how to use these weapons?"

"Yeah, I can," Jason said. "Let's get this stuff loaded in there and go back to your camp."

Kevin wasn't sure about the arrangement yet, but he did feel more secure having someone who seemed to know their way around weapons, had knowledge and, more importantly, a place to go to.

***

Around the fire, Jason told stories of his travels from Las Vegas. He gave stirring details of fighting off both ferals and people, noting that desperate people were just as dangerous.

Kevin could only listen for so long. He got up and went to Paul's tent. "Knock, knock."

"What do you want?" Paul asked.

"We need to talk. Open up," Kevin said.

"I don't want to talk," Paul whined.

"Remember what you told me before Megan died? You said you wanted to start taking a role, taking on responsibility."

"So what? She's dead now. What's the point?" Paul said.

"Let me tell you what's happening. These people—Sabrina, Trent, Ashley—they care but only to the extent that you're willing to help. They feel bad for you, but this old game of people bending over backwards 'cause of your emotions won't fly in this world. The new guy Jason told us the government has retreated, it's just us now, and if you're not going to help, we're not going to help you. I understand you're in pain, I'm hurting too, but Megan would want us to move forward to survive. I promised her I'd look out for you, but you need to also look after yourself. If you're tossing in the cards and don't want to try, then take my Glock and end it all."

Paul didn't answer.

"I'm not being mean, I'm giving you the realities of

the world now. These people will care about you if you care about them. You can't expect people to bend over backwards if you won't reciprocate."

Paul unzipped the tent flap and stepped out. He wiped snot from his nose and said, "You're right."

Kevin furrowed his brow in shock that his words of advice had resonated.

"I miss her," Paul said.

"Me too," Kevin said.

"Who is this new guy?" Paul asked.

"I'm still trying to get a fix on him, but he's some sort of government defense contractor who worked at Nellis Air Force Base in Nevada," Kevin replied.

"I'd like to meet him," Paul said.

"Then let's go introduce you," Kevin said, putting his arm over Paul's shoulders.

"Kevin, I'm sorry I was out of it for a couple of days," Paul said.

"It's fine, but we can't have you or anyone else do that; we all need each other," Kevin said. "That's not to say you can't process a death, but we must toss aside the customs of the past. These are new times."

"It won't happen again," Paul said.

"Glad to hear it. Now let's go huddle up around the fire and have a drink," Kevin said.

CHAPTER SEVEN

SOUTHEAST OF PRESTON, IDAHO

JUNE 6, 2020

With Jason, the group now had a plan. With Faro, Yukon Territory, as their destination, they'd have to travel a distance of over twenty-two hundred miles, much of it in parts of Canada that had no services, meaning no food, water or fuel. If they were going to make such a long journey, they needed to stock up and planned to do so along the way, with their first stop being outside Preston, Idaho.

When dawn's first light hit, they set out. Jason rode with Sabrina, Trent and Ashley, and Paul and Kevin were in the truck.

Jason had already pinpointed stops along his route before losing his vehicle to an attack by marauders south of Bear Lake. It was from there that he'd hiked and run into Sabrina and Kevin.

One stop he had designated was a U-Haul rental facility southeast of Preston, Idaho. There he had planned on getting a trailer for the truck he had so he could load as much supplies as he'd need. The rental facility also had fuel and other items in their rental store they could use.

Jason lowered the binoculars and said, "Looks clear." He handed them to Kevin. "Take a look."

Kevin put the binoculars to his face and scanned the

rental facility, looking for anyone, human or feral. "Yeah, seems to be empty."

"You've got a nice rig," Jason said, eyeballing Kevin's truck.

"It was my girlfriend's; she liked trucks," Kevin said.

"She had good taste," Jason said.

"What happened to your vehicle?" Kevin asked.

"Stolen, the problem when you're traveling alone is you're alone. Short story version is I stopped to take a piss, got jumped; they beat me up and took my truck. She was a beauty too," Jason said. "Just goes to show you can't even trust your instincts. I thought the area where I had pulled over was safe—nope. Also goes to show you that we have as much to fear from non-ferals as ferals."

"How did you get the gear you have now?" Kevin asked.

Jason took the binoculars back from Kevin and replied, "Stole it." He walked off and went back to the car.

Kevin wanted to judge him but refrained on account that everything he'd gotten so far was technically stolen. Although was there a defining line between scavenging and taking what you know someone else needs?

Using a notepad and pen that Paul had found back at the park, Jason sketched the layout of the rental facility. Even though it appeared vacant, it might not be.

"I say we drive in the main entrance, just go for it. Speed will be our friend. Kevin, Paul and I will go in first with the truck. Kevin, you'll drop me at the front; I'll go inside and get a hitch. You'll continue around back—"

"I've been thinking, why not just take a truck? Why are we messing with a trailer?" Paul asked, interrupting Jason.

"We've gone over this already. Your time was then to speak up," Sabrina said.

"I remember, but I've been thinking. Why don't we just take a truck instead?" Paul asked again, ignoring Sabrina's snarky comment.

"We end up spreading the driving among three vehicles versus two," Jason replied.

"Who's driving it, you?" Trent asked.

"Sure," Paul answered.

"But we'll need to have someone else with you; that won't be me," Ashley chimed in.

Kevin shook his head at the nasty comments.

"You know, getting a truck would give us some flexibility," Jason said, thinking over the idea. He'd been stuck on the trailer idea because that was his plan when he only had himself.

"We can load more stuff in one of those smaller box trucks. It just seems more reasonable to take another vehicle if we can versus limiting the truck's capability and performance," Paul said.

"I like it," Jason said.

"Me too," Kevin said, nodding.

"And who's going to drive with him?" Sabrina asked.

"I will," Jason said.

"And what about Kevin?" Sabrina asked.

Ashley and Trent looked at each other.

"Fine, I'll go with him," Trent said.

"Then it's a plan. We go for a box truck instead," Jason said. "Things aren't that different. You'll drop me at the front of the store and drive around back. I'll get the keys and meet you out back. We'll take the truck, pull it up to the back of the store, and start loading. Paul, I'll have you start filling gas cans; you'll find the pumps located near the back of the lot. Sabrina, you and the other two will provide watch at the entrance. Sound good?"

The group nodded.

"Then let's do this," Jason said enthusiastically. "And remember, we get in and out as fast as possible, and radios, make sure they're set to channel two."

"Are you always this chipper?" Sabrina asked.

"I told myself after this shit show began that I'd appreciate life. Yeah, it's hard, but I'm alive, and while I am, I'm going to try to be as positive as I can."

***

Everything was going according to plan. They arrived, got a rental truck with no issues, and had begun filling it with anything of value.

Sabrina, Ashley and Trent took up positions near the entrance off the main road and stood guard.

The facility was south of town and all by itself. Around it lay open land. It was about as perfect a location as they could get. With no neighboring buildings, they didn't have to worry about anyone else.

Out front, Sabrina felt like a bump on a log. She

didn't like that she was left out of the scavenging party. Knowing Paul was allowed to go infuriated her; she had come to find him annoying and, in her own words, lazy and unreliable. What made this situation worse was it was Paul's idea to get the truck versus a trailer, with Jason eventually agreeing. She had broached the idea two days before, but Jason had quickly dismissed it. Was he being sexist? No, she thought. He was levelheaded and reasonable, but why change his mind on the spot, minutes from executing the plan?

A low rumble sounded in the distance.

All three snapped their heads and looked north towards town and saw three trucks heading south along the highway at a high rate of speed.

Sabrina pulled her radio and keyed it. "Jason, we have someone coming down the road towards us."

"How many?" Jason replied.

"Three trucks," Sabrina answered.

Jason stopped what he was doing and walked out of the store to get a better look.

The trucks were close and beginning to slow. It was apparent they were coming to the facility.

"Sabrina, I need all of you to fall back to the store, now, hurry," Jason radioed.

Doing what he ordered, the three jumped into the Subaru and raced back to the store.

"Kev, we have company coming. How good are you with a rifle?" Jason asked.

"Decent," Kevin replied.

"Good, take up a spot behind those trucks to the

right; you'll be our sniper. Where's Paul?" Jason asked, keying his radio. "Paul, I need you to come back to the store ASAP."

Paul heard the call and came running.

With everyone inside the store, minus Kevin, Jason said, "We have to expect that whoever is coming will mean us harm. We need to be prepared to stand our ground."

Everyone nodded and looked determined, except Paul appeared ashen. He'd never been in a fight much less a gunfight. He wasn't even quite sure how to shoot the M16 he'd been given.

They took up positions at the front and waited.

The trucks pulled into the parking lot, one going left, one right, and the other stopping at the center near the front door. About a dozen men poured out of the trucks, all holding various styles of rifles.

"Are we just going to start shooting?" Sabrina asked.

"I don't believe in asking questions, so, yes, on my count—"

"Wait, what if they don't mean us harm?" Paul asked, his hands trembling.

"We can't take a chance, they outnumber us, and our only advantage is surprise. We can get most of them, but it requires shooting fast and accurately," Jason said.

"I don't like this. They might be good people," Paul protested.

A large man with a bolt-action rifle slung over his back approached the Subaru that was parked out front. He touched the hood and said, "It's warm, boys.

Someone is here!"

All the men readied their weapons.

"You three go around back," he hollered to the men to his right. "You go that way," he barked at the others to his left. "You stay out here, and the rest of you, come inside with me."

"We can talk to them," Paul insisted.

"No, Paul, we can't," Jason said.

"Can we shoot?" Sabrina asked, her finger hovering over the trigger of her M16.

"One second. Trent, go to the back and hammer those guys coming around that way," Jason ordered. He keyed his radio and said to Kevin, "Fire when you're ready."

Kevin heard the radio, flipped the selector switch of his M16 to SEMI, placed his finger on the trigger, and took aim on the first man he saw walking around the building towards the back.

"This is a bad idea," Paul said and took off towards the back of the store.

"Where are you going?" Sabrina asked.

"I'm not going to die," Paul whined, disappearing into a back office.

"Coward," Sabrina snapped.

"Forget him. It's showtime," Jason said, taking aim.

The large man who was in charge headed to the front door, reached for it, then stopped when a handheld radio on his belt crackled to life. *"Billy, get back to town. Some of those things were seen near your house."*

Billy froze, pulled the radio from his belt, and keyed

it. "I'll be right there." He whistled and hollered, "Let's go, boys, some of those things are at my house. We need to get back."

"Don't shoot, don't shoot," Jason said, seeing the men were leaving. He keyed his radio and conveyed the message to Kevin, who acknowledged the call.

"But what about whoever is here?" a man asked Billy.

"Don't have time to worry about them. See if they left the keys in their car," Billy said.

Another man opened the door and cried out, "Keys are in it."

"Take it and let's go," Billy ordered, jumping behind the wheel of a truck and slamming the door.

"They're taking our car," Sabrina said.

"Let them go. If we don't have to fight them, we won't," Jason ordered.

"But our car," Sabrina squawked.

"It's fine. We have a truck now," Jason said.

The rumble of the truck engine behind them came to life.

"No, we don't," Trent said from the back of the store.

"We'll find another truck. It's fine. Let them go," Jason said.

The group watched the others leave with their car and the box truck loaded with some equipment.

"This is bullshit," Sabrina cursed. "We should have opened fire. We could have taken them."

"There were twelve of them; our chances weren't a

hundred percent. Best they take a car versus take a life," Jason said, walking to the front desk and fishing for more keys.

"Where's Paul?" Sabrina asked.

Ashley walked into the back office and called out, "He's in here hiding behind a desk. He's curled up like a baby."

Kevin ran into the store and said, "That was close."

Sabrina shouted, "Your fat friend ran off and hid in the back!"

"Huh, what happened?" Kevin asked.

"Paul didn't want to fight. He chose to run and hide," Sabrina blurted out.

Emerging from the back office, Paul came out with his head hung low. After seeing how the events had unfolded, he regretted his actions. "Sorry, guys, I thought we were all going to die."

"You expect us to forgive you for bailing on us?" Sabrina asked.

"I don't want to die," Paul protested.

"Neither do we, but we're willing to fight for our lives, not run away and hide," Sabrina chastised him.

"Paul, is this true?" Kevin asked.

"I got scared," Paul confessed.

Embarrassed, Kevin shook his head and said, "This is on you. I won't defend what you did."

"I've got more keys. Let's go get another truck," Jason said, running out the back door towards the rear lot.

"We shouldn't have let those guys take our car,"

Sabrina complained to Kevin.

"It's gone now, not much to do about it," Kevin said.

"How would you like it if they took Megan's truck?" Sabrina asked.

Kevin thought for a second and replied, "I wouldn't like it, but it's only a truck; I'd get another one."

"Let's see how you feel when it happens," Sabrina snapped.

"What does that mean?" Kevin asked.

"It means what I said, if your truck goes missing, don't start bitching about it," Sabrina said, pushing past Kevin and heading out the back to help Jason.

Paul headed for the door but was stopped by Kevin. "We need to talk."

"I said I was sorry," Paul said.

"That's not good enough. You can't pull that shit, you hear me?" Kevin asked.

Trent and Ashley gave Paul a hard stare and exited the store.

"I just thought there was another way with those guys. Maybe we could have talked to them," Paul said.

"So because you didn't get what you wanted, you decided to run off?" Kevin asked.

"I know what I did was wrong. Stop giving me a hard time," Paul growled.

"You're getting testy with me? I've backed you up all the time. Today, that was unforgiveable. If you want the others to protect you, you have to be willing to protect them, and that means fighting," Kevin reprimanded.

A lower rumble came from out front.

Kevin went and saw two of the trucks had returned. Eight men in total got out and fanned across the front of the property. "Go, out the back, hurry," Kevin said, pushing Paul towards the back door.

Before they could exit, gunfire erupted on the left side of the building.

The front door of the store opened.

Kevin turned and saw two men walk in. He swung around and engaged them by shooting multiple times. He struck both men, but not fatally.

Outside, he found Paul huddled near the box truck along with Sabrina, Trent and Ashley. "Where's Jason?" Kevin asked.

"Don't know," Sabrina replied before taking a few shots from her position towards the left side.

The others were returning fire, striking the side of the box truck.

"Trent, come with me," Kevin said, running along the back wall until he got to the right side. He peeked around and saw three men coming their way. He gave Trent a hand sign indicating what he saw.

Trent replied with a thumbs-up.

"On three—one, two, three," Kevin said and pivoted out, took aim on the men, and started shooting.

Trent followed suit.

The two quickly eliminated the three men.

The sound of a truck sliding came from behind them. It was Jason; he was in Kevin's truck. "Get in!" he shouted from the open driver's window.

Paul didn't hesitate; he ran to the truck and slowly climbed into the bed of the truck. Behind him came Ashley and Sabrina.

"Go," Kevin ordered Trent.

Trent ran and, with one big leap, flew into the bed.

"Kevin, come on!" Jason shouted.

"No, I can take these guys," Kevin shouted.

"Don't be a fool. Get in!" Sabrina shouted.

Those in the bed of the truck were firing back at the men on the left side.

Seeing his reluctance was causing them to remain vulnerable, Kevin gave up on his idea to take out the other few. He ran and leapt into the truck like Trent had.

Jason slammed on the accelerator.

The truck sprayed gravel and rocks, finally gripping the ground and shooting forward.

Not wanting to drive north into town, Jason turned the wheel hard to the right, got onto the southbound lanes, and sped off.

"Anyone hurt?" Sabrina asked.

"I'm good," Trent said.

"Fine," Ashley replied.

"A-ok," Paul said, his thumb raised.

Sabrina rolled her eyes when Paul spoke up.

Kevin looked back at the rental facility. He was thankful they'd gotten away but also saw the entire thing as a wasted opportunity. They were leaving with less than they had begun their day.

NORTHEAST OF WESTON, IDAHO

The group assembled around the campfire, dour looks on all their faces.

Jason, on the other hand, was optimistic as always. "You win some, you lose some."

"Were you a motivational speaker or something?" Trent asked.

"No, but when this is all over, maybe I'll become one." Jason smiled.

"That requires us surviving. After today, I'm not so sure we can," Ashley complained.

"We did fine. Both times we were outnumbered, and the second time, we killed or wounded at least five, and all of us got a way without a scratch," Jason said. "I'd say that's a good day."

"I scratched my knee," Trent quipped.

"Losing my car and not getting what we needed isn't winning, nor is it a good day. It was a shitty day, period," Sabrina complained.

"We'll find you another car, but our next stop is a grain wholesaler just north of here. We go check it out and see if it has what I hope it has, a ton—literally, by the way—a ton of food," Jason said.

"And if it does, we don't have a box truck," Sabrina said.

Jason ignored her snide comments and pulled out a map. He pointed on the map and said, "Just south of Blackrock is a small industrial area. The grain warehouse is here, and just north of that is a cement plant and a gravel pit."

"So?" Sabrina said.

"Meaning there will be trucks. We'll find something big enough to load a bunch of food, and I bet there's fuel at the cement plant. We'll be fine; we just need to keep our heads about us," Jason said confidently. He shot Paul a look and asked him, "What happened today?"

"He pussed out," Trent said.

"Ease up on the name-calling," Kevin said.

"I got scared," Paul confessed.

Jason narrowed his gaze and looked straight into Paul's eyes. "I don't know you, but you can't do that stuff."

"Listen, guys, I've already talked to him about this," Kevin said.

The fire crackled, popped and spit out a hot coal that hit Paul's leg. He scooted away from the fire and wiped the coal away. "He did talk to me. It won't happen again."

"Can you make that a promise?" Jason asked.

"He won't do it again, okay?" Kevin snapped.

Jason threw his hands up in the air and said, "Fair enough."

"When do we ride for that grain warehouse?" Sabrina asked.

"Tomorrow afternoon, let's head up. We'll stash the truck somewhere then go on foot to recon the area and check it out," Jason said. "Kevin, what do you think?"

"Sounds good," Kevin replied.

The group broke up. Ashley and Trent walked off to their tent while Sabrina hung close to the fire. Paul too went to his tent, but Jason called Kevin to come talk. The two walked away from the fire and into the cool evening.

"I know that you were kind of the top dog, so to speak, before I came along. I hope my taking charge of certain things isn't rubbing you the wrong way?" Jason asked.

Kevin thought about his question for a moment and answered, "I'm fine, I'm not good at being bossed around, but you've thought this out. Why wouldn't I let you take the lead?"

"When we get to the warehouse tomorrow, I want you to take charge of the execution of it; that way the group doesn't get confused about who's really in charge," Jason said.

"If you're worried about stepping on toes, don't be. I haven't known the rest of them very long. But if you want me to run our little operation tomorrow, I'd love to," Kevin said.

"Good, I just don't want any hard feelings," Jason said and patted Kevin on the shoulder. "Say, your friend Paul. Is he good?"

"Yeah, he's good."

"Just that tomorrow we can't have him doing that again. Maybe give him a responsibility he can't run from like being on overwatch," Jason suggested.

"I'll think about it," Kevin said.

"That reminds me," Jason said. "Follow me."

Jason led Kevin to his truck. He rummaged through a large duffel in the back and produced a bolt-action rifle. "Give Paul this instead of the rifle he had. He didn't look confident about handling the M16."

"I'll let him have it, thanks," Kevin said.

Again Jason patted Kevin on the shoulder. "You're a good guy; I like you."

"Thanks," Kevin said. He didn't want to say the same about Jason, as he still wasn't quite sure about him.

"I'm going to hit the sack; I have third shift. You'd best get some shut-eye too," Jason suggested then walked off, leaving Kevin next to his truck in the bright moonlight.

Kevin gave the rifle a once-over. It was a nice rifle; he just hoped Paul would be fine with changing out.

Having Jason give him the lead tomorrow did make him feel better, though he was never that type of person that became upset from not being in charge. He wasn't afraid of leading and would if it was needed; but when Jason came on the scene, he'd definitely taken a step back, seeing that Jason knew what he was doing.

He agreed with Sabrina that today was a total failure but differed with her, as he thought each day provided an opportunity to turn it all around. Her constant complaining and bickering dissipated what allure she'd had for him. It was evident she had her eyes on Jason, and for him that was fine. After Megan, he wasn't sure how long it would take for him to ever feel for someone again. When a normal relationship had a breakup, it could be tough; but losing the love of your life to death was something totally different.

He pushed those thoughts from his mind and put his focus on the plan going successfully tomorrow, because failure wasn't an option.

CHAPTER EIGHT

SOUTH OF BLACKROCK, IDAHO

JUNE 9, 2020

Kevin, with the others in tow, emerged from the dry cornstalks at the edge of the road. Like a perfectly choreographed maneuver, they swiftly moved into positions opposite a large warehouse.

Kevin promptly pulled out a set of night-vision goggles and placed them to his face. His eyes carefully scanned the building, paying close attention to doors and windows. The full moon helped illuminate the grainy green view of their target, the C & J Food Company, a large distributor of grains and beans. "It looks clear," Kevin whispered.

"I think we need to reconsider this," Paul replied, his tone indicating fear. He sat with his back plastered to an abandoned truck, his hands clenching the bolt-action rifle Kevin had given him

"We agreed nighttime provides us cover," Kevin argued.

"But those things, what if they can see in the dark?" Paul countered.

Kevin ignored Paul. He squatted down, pulled out a radio and keyed it. "Everyone ready?"

One by one, the others replied, "Yes."

Kevin turned to Paul. With an outstretched arm, he

handed him the night-vision goggles. "Keep an eye on us."

"Kevin, listen, this is a bad idea," Paul again protested.

"Bro, we got this. We've been watching this place for a solid day, no movement, nothing. I think it's clear."

"Let's give it another day," Paul whined.

"No. Now is the time. Plus, I'm starving for something other than MREs. If this place hasn't been touched, this will be a gold mine, the proverbial mother lode of food," Kevin replied.

"It just doesn't feel right," Paul groaned.

"Get your shit together, man. You're our eyes and ears out here," Kevin said.

"We're ready. What's the holdup?" Sabrina radioed.

Kevin patted Paul on the shoulder and asked, "You good?"

Paul nodded.

Kevin keyed the radio, "On the count of three, I'll lead the way to the front door. Ashley and Jason, go around back. Trent, Sabrina, you're with me." He gave Paul one more assuring look and began the countdown. "One, two, three."

On cue, Ashley and Jason bolted from their hide position and across the street towards the left side of the warehouse.

Kevin, with his M16 in hand, took off for the front entrance, a set of glass doors.

Sabrina and Trent were close behind Kevin.

Paul got to his knees and watched as his friends

raced off. The light from the moon enabled him to see perfectly.

Kevin reached the front doors. The others stacked up behind him. He looked over his shoulder and asked, "What are the odds this is unlocked?"

"Two to one, it's not," Trent joked.

"I'll take that bet. My money's on that it'll open." Sabrina chuckled.

Kevin reached out and grasped the cold metal handle. He paused, said a quick prayer and pulled.

The door opened.

"Pay up, bitch," Sabrina said, elbowing Trent.

"Fine, whatever, pure luck, nothing else," Trent scoffed.

Kevin opened the door slightly and peered into pure darkness. "Hmm," he grunted as he closed the door.

"What's wrong?" Sabrina asked.

"It's dark as hell in there. I can't see a thing," Kevin replied.

"Here, toss this inside. See if it stirs up anything," Trent said, passing Kevin a rock.

Kevin took the rock, opened the door again, and chucked the rock in. It banged loudly off something metallic before hitting the tile floor with a loud smack. Kevin listened intently. Nothing moved. Silence.

"That's a good sign," Sabrina said.

"Kevin, we're at the back door. It's locked," Jason radioed.

"Stay put. Front door is open; we're going inside. We'll let you in. Until then, keep eyes on that side for us," Kevin replied. He craned his head back and asked, "You guys ready?"

"Yep, let's go," Trent said.

Sabrina nodded.

Kevin pulled out a flashlight and held it in his left hand. He slung his rifle, unholstered his Glock 17 and readied himself. "No better time than the present," he said and headed inside.

***

Paul's hand shook, and a cold sweat clung to his brow. It had been almost seven minutes and nothing from the others. The urge to radio them was gnawing at him, but Kevin had given specific orders not to unless it was an emergency.

"C'mon, guys, where are you?" he mumbled under his breath.

A cool wind from the north sent shivers down his spine. Although he was a native of Utah, he disliked the cold, and for him that meant anything under sixty degrees.

A loud clang echoed off in the distance.

He looked through the night vision in the direction of the sound. Slowly he scanned the area, but saw nothing. But he had heard something; that wasn't his imagination. *A cat, maybe a dog*, he thought.

Growing impatient, he hit the light on his watch. It was four seventeen.

Kevin and the others had been gone for almost ten minutes.

A clacking sound came from the same area he'd heard the clang. He put the night vision back to his face and looked. This time he saw movement, but it was hard to tell what it was through the grainy lens of the old-generation night vision.

"Argh, these things suck," he grumbled.

The clacking grew louder. Whatever it was, it was getting closer.

***

"Holy shit, look at all this food!" Kevin yelped, his arms held over his head in a sign of excitement.

With her mouth stuffed, Sabrina smiled and said, "Sooo good."

"What do you have there?" Trent asked, the beam of his light on her.

"Dude, you're blinding me," Sabrina snapped.

"Sorry, what you got there?" he asked.

"Rice crackers," she said, holding out the box.

He took it and shoved his hand deep inside.

Stuffing her mouth with a handful, she purred, "They're the best rice crackers I've ever had."

"Twenty-one, twenty-two, twenty-three…" Kevin said happily, counting the pallets.

"Has anyone contacted Paul?" Jason asked.

"Not yet," Kevin replied.

Jason turned to the others, who were busy going through the boxes.

They all shook their heads.

"Poor guy, we're in here celebrating and stuffing our faces, and he's out there probably shitting his pants." Jason laughed.

"Kev, where did you find that guy?" Ashley asked as she pulled the plastic sheeting off a pallet of boxed cereal.

"Give it a break. Paul's a good guy. You all give him such a hard time. And, Ashley, you know he's my girlfriend's brother, so knock it off with the cliché and snarky remarks," Kevin replied.

"The fact you gave him the job of watching over us is scary." Trent laughed.

Kevin turned to face the group. "Guys, he needs to find a purpose. He's got some good senses, he's fine."

"Like the other day?" Ashley mocked.

"Give him time; he might surprise you. He's shocked me a few times," Kevin said.

"Kev, he up and ran off. Ash found him cowering in the fetal position," Trent snapped, referring to the Preston situation.

Kevin stepped forward. "Paul has his faults. We all do."

"Yeah, but his could get us killed," Sabrina quipped.

"Enough Paul bashing, he's a person, a human being, and right now, there's not a lot of us around anymore. As far as making sure he's up for the challenge, how about talking to him, getting his skills honed. He's not a star athlete like you, Trent, or an astrophysicist like you, Ashley. Unfortunately, he's just a store clerk, who didn't have the advantages you had, Sabrina; going to Stanford to become a chemist wasn't an option for him. But he's part of our team now. I gave him that job to let him know he's one of us. He needs to build confidence, but if all we do is make snide comments and bully him, he'll never be an effective part of the team. So just drop it. He's fine out there; he has our back," Kevin blared.

***

Paul sank down and scooted underneath the truck once he identified the sound was ferals running down the paved street towards him.

His heart was thumping loudly in his chest, so much he worried they could hear him.

Three ferals paused their advance. With their heads craned high in the air, they sniffed.

Paul gulped. His mind began to question his decision to hide under the truck versus making a run for it. *Can they smell me?* Unsure of their full range of senses, he knew their hearing was keen. The last thing he needed was for the radio to begin blaring. He slowly reached down and clicked the handheld off.

A single feral snapped its head towards the truck.

Paul pressed his eyes closed. His temples pulsed and sweat beaded on his brow. *Did it hear that?*

The feral stepped towards the truck. Its head swiveled as it sniffed loudly, its teeth chattering incessantly the entire time.

It knows I'm here, fuck, it knows I'm here. His mind began to play out his own grisly death.

With incredible agility, the feral leapt onto the roof

of the truck, its weight making the shocks of the truck squeak.

Terror overcame Paul. Unable to control his basic human functions, he began to urinate on himself.

The other two ferals turned towards the truck as the smell of urine hit their nostrils.

Tears welled in Paul's eyes. This was it. This was how he would die. His shaking hand gripped his rifle. Feeling the wood of the stock, he then decided if he was going to die, at least he'd go out fighting. If today would be his last, he'd die with some sense of dignity.

The feral on the roof began to slither down the side of the truck.

With two coming from the left side and the other feral coming from the other, Paul was surrounded. He needed to make his move now or never. He moved his rifle towards the right side and leveled it in the direction he guessed the feral would appear. When it did, he'd fire. This, he hoped, would kill it and give him the chance to flee.

Gingerly the one feral inched down the side of the truck. It was as if it was toying with Paul for maximum psychological effect. The other two squatted down, no doubt they could see him now, but they had stopped their advance. They were waiting on the other. This attack was tactical, showing a sign of intelligence.

Paul waited for the feral to show itself. The terror he'd felt at first was gone, replaced by a deep resolve to fight. Resigned to his fate, he told himself that if he could take one with him, then the war against the ferals was still even, one human for one feral, a draw.

***

"I can't reach him. He's not replying," Sabrina said, holding her radio in frustration.

"Did he run off and leave us again?" Trent cracked.

"I bet he didn't replace the batteries in his radio." Ashley laughed.

"Jason, can you go out and check on him, make sure he's alright, and let him come in. Take his place on watch," Kevin ordered.

"Fine," Jason groaned, grabbing his rifle and heading to the front door. "Don't eat all the Toasty O's."

"How about we find a secure place to rest for the day? Go lock the back door," Kevin said to Ashley. He turned to Trent and ordered, "Head up to the second level; see what's up there."

Jason reached the front door and paused when faint laughter came from within the warehouse. He frowned. His friends were having fun and celebrating their success while he had to go and ensure Paul could do the most basic responsibilities of all, provide watch. A sweet laugh hit his ears; it was Sabrina. He'd noticed earlier she had her eye on him. He liked her and it appeared she liked him. A smile creased his face as he imagined them together. What they needed was some time alone.

With his mind somewhere else, he exited the warehouse.

***

Any moment, the lone feral's head would appear, and then Paul would take his shot, a shot that would likely be his last.

The front door of the warehouse opened.

The two ferals whipped around and spotted an unaware Jason. They bolted towards him.

The sound of their heavy footfalls tore Jason away from his arousing thoughts of Sabrina. He started to raise his rifle, but it was too late.

Both ferals tackled him to the ground.

The lone feral back at the truck made its move. It jumped down on all fours and shrieked.

Paul was ready and pulled the trigger. The high-velocity bullet struck it in the face and exited with explosive force out the back of its head. Without a sound, it fell to the ground, dead.

Jason screamed in pain as the two ferals savagely ripped him apart.

***

The screams and gunshot were heard by all inside.

"Jason!" Sabrina cried out as she ran for the front door.

"Sabrina, wait. We don't know what's going on out there!" Kevin hollered.

"What do you think is going on!" she snapped.

"Ashley, is the back secure?" Kevin asked.

"Yes," Ashley confirmed.

"Trent, what's the status up there?" Kevin asked.

"We can barricade ourselves up here. It's a solid defensible position," Trent replied from a catwalk elevated above Kevin.

"Ashley, go upstairs. You and Trent hide. I'll go help Sabrina," Kevin said, running off.

***

Paul scooted out from underneath the truck and stood. He took a step but found his legs were wobbly.

Jason's screams ceased.

The ferals continued to rip and tear at Jason's battered body.

Paul raised his rifle and cycled the bolt.

One of the ferals heard the distinct sound of the bolt action and turned towards Paul.

Without hesitation, Paul squeezed the trigger. The bullet exploded out the muzzle and struck the feral in the chest.

It howled and clutched the wound.

The second feral swung around and ran towards Paul, but its advance was hampered by a volley of gunfire from Sabrina's M16. It crashed to the ground but wasn't dead. It dug its fingers into the gravel of the parking lot and dragged itself towards Paul.

Paul cycled the bolt and finished the job by placing a round in its head.

Sabrina ran up to Jason's body. Alongside it, the feral

clung to life, its breathing labored and blood oozing from the wound on its chest. Unforgiving, Sabrina leveled the barrel of her rifle at its face and pulled the trigger.

Paul stood frozen in the street. He had survived the assault, but his team had suffered the loss of Jason.

Kevin ran out of the front and towards them. "Are we clear?"

Paul didn't reply. He just stood, his feet anchored to the pavement and his stare fixed on Sabrina with her arms cradled around Jason's body.

Kevin came up and looked down on the gruesome scene. "Is he...?"

"Yes," Sabrina replied, her voice trembling.

"Paul, you okay?" Kevin asked.

Paul didn't reply.

"Paul! Are you hurt?" Kevin asked.

Sabrina's sadness turned to anger. She gently put Jason's head down and stood up. Not saying a word, she marched over to Paul and punched him in the face.

Paul reeled from the strike. He tripped over his own feet and fell down.

"Sabrina, what are you doing?"

"He didn't warn us, nothing. He could have warned us, warned Jason. But he didn't. He probably hid and let those things come!" Sabrina barked.

Paul lay on the ground, rubbing his jaw. Still he had nothing to say.

Kevin looked around. Soon the sun would be rising, and after all the gunfire, more ferals could be coming. "We need to get inside, now."

"Damn you!" Sabrina yelled, kicking Paul's leg.

"Enough, get inside," Kevin ordered.

"What about Jason's body?" Sabrina asked.

"You know the drill; he lies where he dies. Now come on before more of those things show up."

Sabrina walked over to Jason's body and whispered, "Goodbye, see you on the other side." Wiping tears from her face, she briskly headed to the warehouse.

Kevin approached Paul. "You good?" he asked with his arm outstretched.

"I, um, I couldn't radio. They came up too fast. I-I, um, thought they'd just keep going, but..." Paul mumbled.

"Never mind, we'll discuss this all later. Now get up, come on," Kevin said.

Paul took Kevin's hand.

Once on his feet, Kevin could smell the strong stench of urine. He thought about saying something, but now wasn't the time. They hurried inside and joined the others.

CHAPTER NINE

SOUTH OF BLACKROCK, IDAHO

JUNE 10, 2020

Paul couldn't sleep. He tried, but it was fruitless. The trauma from the attack was too much. Every time he closed his eyes, all he could see was the pasty gruesome face of the feral shrieking at him.

Sabrina also remained awake, her gaze fixed on Paul with hate-filled eyes.

Trent and Ashley didn't have any trouble sleeping while Kevin remained awake to provide security and make sure Sabrina didn't attack Paul again.

The remaining hours of night brought bone-chilling sounds from outside the warehouse. There was no need for explanation, Kevin knew what it was.

The sun's orange rays came streaming in through a long row of windows perched near the ceiling. It was a welcome sight for Kevin, as now he'd be able to catch a few hours of sleep. He leaned over and tapped Trent's leg. "Hey, get up. Your turn."

Trent rolled over but kept sleeping.

Kevin tapped harder and raised his voice. "Trent, it's your shift."

"Let him sleep. I'll take his watch," Sabrina offered.

Kevin grinned and replied, "No. You've been up all night too, and when I wake, I'd like to find Paul alive."

"Huh?" Trent mumbled, rubbing his eyes.

"It's morning; sun's up. Your turn for watch," Kevin said.

Trent sat up and stretched. He looked at everyone and groaned, "Everyone is awake, and you're waking me up?"

"Do I need to explain? Go take a piss, and when you come back, you're on watch," Kevin said.

Trent mumbled something unintelligible and sauntered off.

Sabrina jumped up and came over to Kevin. "Can we talk?"

"Sure," Kevin replied.

She plopped down next to him and whispered, "You need to find out what happened last night."

"I will."

"You must or…"

"Or what?" Kevin snapped.

"I talked with Trent and Ashley; they agree."

"Agree with what?"

"If Paul was negligent or cowardly, there must be consequences," Sabrina stated.

"What would you like me to do? Hold a trial, and if he's guilty, take him out and shoot him?" Kevin mocked.

Sabrina leaned in and said, "We all work well together, we're a team, but if one person is not doing their part, we don't function. In fact, it can be dangerous, deadly even, like we saw last night."

Kevin patted her on the arm and said, "When Trent gets back, I'm going to take a nap. When I get up, we'll discuss it more."

"No, when Trent gets back, you need to question Paul on exactly what happened last night. I can't wait any longer."

Trent lumbered up the stairwell, his hand sliding along the worn metal railing.

"Wake Ashley," Sabrina ordered Trent.

"For what?" Trent asked.

"We're going to get the truth about what happened last night," Sabrina answered.

"Can't this wait?" Trent asked.

Ashley yawned and said, "I'm already awake. Go ahead."

Sabrina turned to Kevin and glared. "Everyone is up."

Kevin sighed heavily. "I'm tired; can't this wait?"

"Jason died. We need to know, now," Sabrina insisted.

"I'm with Sabrina. Let's see what dopey has to say," Trent mocked.

"Enough name-calling, Trent, we're a team. Shit happens," Kevin said.

"I think you're overly defensive of Paul because he's your dead girlfriend's brother," Ashley snarked.

Kevin nodded his head in disgust.

The entire time, Paul sat and listened, but when his sister was mentioned, he perked up. "Don't talk about Megan."

"There's the peanut gallery. How about you tell us what happened last night," Sabrina said, shifting to look at Paul squarely.

Kevin stood up and barked, "Stop, this needs to stop!"

Everyone grew quiet and stared at Kevin.

"Apparently this couldn't wait," Kevin said, looking at each person before settling his gaze on Paul. "What happened last night? Why didn't you radio about the ferals?"

"It all happened so fast. I first heard this odd sound. I wasn't sure what it was. I looked, and just like that, they were feet from me. If I had radioed you, they would have spotted me and killed me."

"Better you than Jason," Sabrina quipped.

Kevin pointed a stiff finger and snapped, "Enough!"

"I thought they'd just pass by, you know, like they were heading somewhere else."

"Did you turn your radio off?" Kevin asked.

"Yes."

"Why?" Kevin asked.

"Like I said, I thought they'd just pass by. If I radioed, they would have heard me and then—"

"And then Jason would be alive," Sabrina snapped.

"Seriously, enough, can I get to the bottom of this?" Kevin scolded.

"But I was wrong. They didn't pass by; they somehow knew I was there and began to stalk me. Next thing I know, Jason comes out. Two of the three jumped him. I killed the third," Paul explained.

"If you'd warned us—" Sabrina said.

"Sabrina, I won't tell you again; stop interrupting,"

Kevin said.

"Screw this. This fat, lazy slug got Jason killed. All he needed to do was warn us. He couldn't even do that. He can't be part of this team anymore. I don't trust him," Sabrina roared.

Kevin looked at her then towards Ashley and Trent. "You guys feel the same way?"

They both nodded in agreement.

"We agreed that we needed a unanimous decision on things like this. I say no. What he says makes practical sense. He thought they were passing through, but they didn't. We don't know that if he had alerted us, Jason and I wouldn't be dead along with Paul. You've seen those things, they're lethal. We're lucky as hell we took those things out so easily last night," Kevin said. He sighed and continued, "It was a tragic mistake, nothing more. Paul's intentions weren't devious. He decided on the spot and shit happened. It's like how Megan was killed. We make choices, and sometimes those choices result in a fatality. Last night it just happened to be Jason."

"You're siding with this fat fuck?" Sabrina barked.

Paul sank down further and put his head in his hands. He felt horrible about what had happened, and in retrospect, he wished he had just radioed.

"Stop the childish name-calling," Kevin said.

"I'm out. I can't do this anymore," Sabrina said, throwing her arms into the air.

Kevin shook his head and sighed. "C'mon, guys, I know we haven't been together for a long time, but we work well together. We have a plan, let's see it through.

You can't bail on me and Paul now. If we're going to survive against those things, we need numbers."

Ashley gathered her personal belongings and stuffed them into her backpack.

"Ashley, you're leaving?" Kevin asked.

"I'm with Sabrina. Paul is...well, I'll just put it frankly, he's a liability. I need to make it through this; I must make it through this. He messes up everywhere we go, and now it's cost Jason his life," Ashley replied.

Kevin looked at Trent.

He grinned and said, "I'm with the ladies, sorry, bro."

Sabrina approached Kevin and placed her hand gently on his shoulder. "Come with us. Dump the baggage. I know you feel a loyalty to him because of Megan, but she's dead."

"I can't," Kevin said, shaking his head.

Sabrina looked over her shoulder at Paul, who was sulking in the corner. "He's gonna get you killed."

"Where are you guys going?" Kevin asked.

"The Yukon, like we've planned all along, but first I need to go see if my relatives are still alive in Twin Falls."

"You'll need wheels," Kevin said, reminding her that the truck was his.

"I know," Sabrina said.

"There's plenty around. Take your pick," Kevin said. "Listen, you're making a mistake. Don't be so hasty; let's see this through."

"No, you are," Sabrina said.

A screeching howl came from outside, near the

parking lot.

Everyone went silent; their eyes widened.

"Ferals!" Kevin said with urgency, grabbing his rifle.

Trent ran down the catwalk to a strip of windows that overlooked the street and the parking lot. He peeked out and saw two ferals examining the remains of Jason and the dead ferals. They darted back and forth between the bodies, their heads bobbing up and down as they smelled around and scanned the area. "I see two of them. They're near the bodies from last night. Wait, hold on. They're coming towards the front doors."

Banging sounded on the glass front doors.

Kevin, Sabrina, Ashley and Paul all readied themselves, rifles in hand. From their positions on the second-floor loft, they'd be able to bring concentrated fire upon anything that came into their field of view.

Scratching came from the back door.

"Trent, did they move to the back?" Kevin called out.

"I can't tell. I lost sight of them when they went to the front," he replied, running down the catwalk to a panel of windows that looked down on the backyard. He peered out. "It's the same two. It's like they're casing the place. And they're gone, they took off."

"Stay on lookout. Ashley, go to the front windows and post there," Kevin ordered, naturally falling back into his position as team leader.

Sabrina stepped up to Kevin and nudged him.

He looked at her and said, "I suggest you hold off on leaving until nightfall."

"Yeah, that's what I was going to say," she said. "Listen, about all of this, I'm sorry. I hate to leave you in this position, but I feel strongly—"

"There's no need to apologize. I like you, a lot; you're a natural leader. You'll be fine; we'll be fine. It's just I find it harder to survive out there with fewer numbers. Hell, those things run in packs sometimes; even they know the importance of hanging together."

She leaned close and whispered, "Kev, I don't trust him. I don't. Something tells me not to. You know that whole woman's intuition thing."

Kevin shot a look to Paul, who was still kneeling behind the railing, his rifle in his shoulder. "He's just quirky is all. I've known him for about a year. He's not a bad guy, just odd."

"Please reconsider," Sabrina urged.

"I made a promise to Megan. I won't leave him," Kevin replied.

"I understand, you're a man of your word. I respect that," she said, rubbing his arm.

"I need some sleep. At nightfall, we'll all leave to go to the truck so you can get your stuff," Kevin said. The truck was parked in a hidden location not a mile away.

"Sounds good. Go get some shut-eye," Sabrina said and quickly embraced him.

He returned the embrace but was stunned she had done it. "What was that for?"

"I'm just going to miss you, that's all."

"I didn't really say, but I'm sorry about Jason. I know you two—"

"I'm sorry too, but that's the world we live in now," she replied, fighting back tears. "Go…go lie down. Get some rest," she said, pushing him away.

He watched her walk off, her hand wiping tears away. He turned back to see Paul staring at him. "What?"

"Nothing," Paul answered.

"Then why the hard stare?" Kevin asked.

Ensuring no one was in earshot, Paul said, "Don't trust them."

"Why?"

"Just don't. They've been whispering to each other a lot lately, well before this," Paul said.

Not in the mood to hear conspiracy theories, Kevin simply said, "I've always had a healthy skepticism, don't worry."

"Good."

"Are you tired?" Kevin asked.

"No, I'm good," Paul said, standing up.

With a leery eye towards Sabrina below, Kevin said to Paul, "I need you to be my eyes while I sleep. If you feel tired at all, wake me. In fact, wake me for anything, okay?"

"Okay," Paul said. "I'll wake you for anything, I promise."

***

Kevin opened his eyes. The space around him was filled with an orange glow. It was late afternoon. He had slept ten hours without interruption. He shot up and looked around the loft. In the far corner he saw Paul lying curled up and snoring loudly. His eyes darted to the other corners of the area, but no one else was there. He jumped up and looked over the railing, but the others weren't on the ground floor either.

"Paul, get up!" Kevin barked, rushing towards him. Out of the corner of his eye, he spotted a piece of paper rolled up and shoved in the trigger guard of his rifle. He grabbed it and unrolled it. His eyes widened in shock as he read it.

Paul, groggy from his long nap, slowly sat up. He rubbed his eyes and asked, "What time is it?"

Kevin crumpled the paper in his hands, snatched his rifle and raced down the stairs.

Shocked, Paul jumped to his feet. "What's going on?"

"They took the truck!" Kevin replied as he hit the ground floor and sprinted towards the front doors.

Paul ran after him.

Kevin burst from the entrance and raced towards the cornfield.

Frantic, Paul was close behind. Outside, he began to scan the area, looking for any sign of ferals.

Without concern, Kevin tore through the dry stalks. His anger overcame any concern. He couldn't let them take the truck. In it was everything they needed to survive on the road. Tools and ammunition were the main things he was concerned about losing, but what also angered him was the fact the truck was Megan's. It was the last physical memory he had of her.

Paul's heart felt like it was going to explode. Even after weeks on the road, with limited food, he hadn't lost much weight. His belly bounced with each footfall and his face was bright red.

Kevin exited the cornfield and cursed loudly when he saw the truck was gone. "Shit!" Anger turned to rage; he kicked and threw whatever was in front of him.

Paul emerged and instantly fell to his knees. He gasped and coughed for air.

Seeing Paul, Kevin snapped, "I asked you to do one simple thing, stay up and keep watch!"

Coughing, Paul managed to spit out, "I'm sorry."

"Sorry doesn't cut it. We lost all our gear, water, ammo and the truck!" Kevin bellowed.

"Bro, I'm sorry. I don't know what happened," Paul whined.

Kevin paced the dry flattened grasses, kicking any rock he came upon.

Paul got to his feet. He walked towards Kevin. "We can find another car. There are abandoned cars everywhere."

Kevin clenched his jaw, veins in his neck throbbing with anger. "Sabrina was right. You're a fuckup, a total fuckup."

"I'm sorry."

"No more apologies, that was your last chance, you understand?" Kevin scolded.

Paul nodded.

Kevin brushed by Paul, bumping his shoulder, and marched back into the cornfield.

Paul turned around and asked, "Where are you going?"

"To find another truck."

***

The sun's warm rays were gone, but its light still cast from behind the rolling western sky.

Frustrated and tired, Kevin, with Paul in tow, walked back to the warehouse. Their plan was to lock themselves in for the night and get back to looking for a truck first thing in the morning.

Each time Kevin thought of Sabrina, an anger welled up inside him. From an early age, he'd prided himself on having few friends, but those friends were the type he'd could call upon at any hour and they'd be there. He'd thought Sabrina was one of those people. Their time together was short, but the intensity of life on the road tended to accelerate the process of friendship, you either knew or you didn't. With Sabrina, he'd found a person who was reliable, strong, and intelligent and, up until this morning, trustworthy. His anger didn't stem only from disappointment and betrayal, but heartbreak. How could someone he considered a friend do that?

The hours in between waking until now were filled with countless pleas for forgiveness from Paul.

After the twenty-third *I'm sorry*, Kevin told him to be quiet. The past was the past; their energy needed to be focused on finding another form of reliable transportation.

Inside the warehouse, Kevin headed for the first pallet of cereal. He pulled two boxes of sugared wheat flakes and went to the loft.

Paul did as Kevin had, grabbed a box and followed him to the second-floor loft.

Lost in thought, Kevin didn't notice Paul was right behind him until he sat down and saw Paul climbing the stairs. "Did you lock the doors?"

"Ah, no, sorry, forgot," Paul mumbled. He quickly turned around and raced back to the front door.

Kevin shook his head in disgust.

Minutes later, Paul emerged and began the ascent.

"Paul, you have to get your shit together. You know the last person in always secures the access. We've been doing it that way for weeks," Kevin said just before stuffing his mouth with cereal.

"I forgot, sorry," Paul replied.

"No more apologies, just do it!" Kevin snapped.

"I'll try harder, I promise," Paul said.

"I'll take first watch. You get some rest," Kevin said.

"But I'm not tired," Paul complained.

"When we decide to sleep, I've got first watch, okay?" Kevin clarified.

Like an awkward child, Paul was all thumbs opening the cereal. After several failed attempts to open the bag, he pulled with force. The bag exploded open, flakes flying everywhere.

Kevin shook his head in disbelief. Sabrina was right, Paul was a screwup. He wanted to hate the man, but each time he'd think poorly of him, he could hear Megan's sweet last words pleading with Kevin to take care of her baby brother. Being a man of his word, he'd fulfill that request to the best of his ability.

CHAPTER TEN

SOUTH OF BLACKROCK, IDAHO

JUNE 11, 2020

Kevin woke. He blinked repeatedly, but the darkness that surrounded him prevented him from seeing.

A rumbling came from outside. It sounded like the throaty exhaust of a vehicle.

He shot up and reached for where he remembered putting his rifle; his hands found it.

"Psst, Paul, wake up," he said.

No response.

Using his flashlight, he flashed over in the direction where Paul slept but found he wasn't there. *Is he downstairs on watch?*

The rumbling and popping of the engine stopped.

Kevin leaned over the railing of the loft. "Paul, where are you?" he called out just above a whisper.

Still no response.

Kevin listened intently. He could hear the distinct sound of feet crunching gravel just outside the back door. He put his rifle to his shoulder and placed his cheek against the rear stock. If someone was coming through that door, he was going to put an end to them.

The ferals were their top adversary, but marauding humans came in a close second.

The back door creaked open.

How is that possible? Kevin thought, remembering he'd locked it himself just before ending his watch hours ago. *Could it be?* Being a man who shot and asked questions later, he placed his finger on the trigger and began to apply pressure. He couldn't see, but he was at least pointed in the general direction of the threat.

Click. A light streaked across the ground floor.

The bright white LED illuminated the space and gave Kevin a clear shot.

He looked through his optics but paused when he identified the trespasser. "Paul?"

Paul swung the flashlight towards the loft, blinding Kevin. "Yeah."

Shielding his eyes with his left hand, Kevin asked, "What are you doing?"

"Sorry, I, um, felt so bad about you losing the truck that I decided to go look for one."

Kevin headed down the stairs.

"I was going to wake you, but I know you needed the sleep. Anyway, I remembered seeing this old house a half mile or so back along the county road. I thought maybe there's a car there; well, there was," he said, motioning with his finger towards the back lot, where the truck was now parked.

Kevin marched towards Paul.

Unsure of his intentions, Paul took a step back. "Sorry I didn't wake you, but I also didn't want to get us both killed. I figured I needed to, you know, take the risk since I fucked up."

Stopping inches from Paul, Kevin stood stoically.

"Are you mad?" Paul asked sheepishly.

A smiled cracked on Kevin's heavily stubbled face. "How can I be mad now? You got us a truck."

"A cool one too, it's like some hot-rod-type oldie." Paul glowed.

Kevin could see Megan's eyes in Paul's. There could be no doubt they were related. He put his hand on Paul's shoulder and said, "Let's go look at *our* new truck."

EAST OF CHUBBUCK, IDAHO

Kevin weaved around the few abandoned cars at the intersection, keeping an eye out for any threat, human or feral.

"Looks clear," Paul said, gazing out the side window down the long road that led north.

"From the bodies strewn around, it appears these people were attacked. Keep your eyes peeled for anything unusual," Kevin warned as he moved the truck around the rotting corpses and debris.

"You're gonna hate me, but I have to go to the bathroom," Paul said, grimacing.

"Once we're clear of this, say a half mile up, I'll pull over," Kevin said, his eyes fixed on navigating the tight turns through the wreckage that partially blocked his path.

"I was kinda hoping for a toilet."

Clear of the intersection, Kevin slammed on the accelerator. The truck lurched forward. "Clear road ahead."

"Um, did you hear me?" Paul asked.

"Yeah, I did, but I don't want to waste time looking for a pearly white toilet. Just piss outside the truck. In fact, I think there's an empty bottle behind the seat. Just fill it up and toss it out," Kevin said, pointing behind him.

"I don't need to pee." Paul winced.

Kevin gave Paul a look and said, "Oh, well, just take a dump on the side of the road. I don't want to waste more time than we have already."

"There's no toilet paper," Paul complained.

Paul's mention of toilet paper brought the other luxuries now long lost to mind. "Listen, I'll find a reasonable place to stop. Just give it a bit. If you're going to shit yourself, please let me know though."

"I'm fine, but I can't hold it forever."

A slight grin appeared on Kevin's face. He looked at Paul and asked, "What's the one thing you miss the most?"

"You mean since the outbreak?" Paul asked.

"Yeah, since civilization came to a screeching halt. What's the one thing you miss the most?"

"Ice cream, rocky road ice cream. Wait, I'll change that, banana fro yo from my local frozen yogurt shop. That stuff was so good. It was creamy, like a custard, really. Simply the best fro yo I've ever had," Paul answered with a big grin.

"Sounds awesome," Kevin said.

"Oh, it was. Whenever Megan would come to my place, I'd take her there. She loved the—"

"Tart with fresh strawberries and blueberries," Kevin interrupted.

"Yep, that's it, her fave."

Both men grew silent for a bit. Thoughts of Megan swirled around in their heads.

Breaking the silence, Paul asked, "And you? What do you miss?"

"I have a tie between pizza and coffee. There was this place a few miles from the house, their pizza was the best. Thin crust, so crispy. God, I can taste it now."

"Yum." Paul smiled.

"But I also miss my morning ritual, getting up and making a large cup of dark roast coffee. I'd add a tiny bit of cream; it was perfect."

"That I could do without," Paul said. "I never liked coffee. I always thought the ritual of it sounded fun and the smell is so great, but I find them all so bitter, even if I sweeten them, just not my cup of tea."

"You mean coffee," Kevin joked.

"Ha, exactly."

"What I'd do for a cup of hot coffee right now," Kevin said, his mind reminiscing about his mornings.

"I feel that way about Mountain Dew," Paul quipped.

"Gross," Kevin said.

"That's how I feel about coffee, so there," Paul fired back.

"I'll tell you what, wherever we go, keep an eye out for coffee, and I'll do the same for Mountain Dew," Kevin said.

"Deal," Paul said, laughing. He spotted something and barked, "There! Right there!" Paul pointed at a house along the side of the road.

Kevin slowed the truck as they approached.

Signage indicated the house was now being used for a quilting and fabric store.

Always cautious, Kevin pulled the truck over and stopped a few hundred feet away. "See anything out of sorts?"

"I see some sheds and a detached garage in the back, but it looks…abandoned," Paul said.

Kevin tapped the accelerator; the truck inched forward. "Looks approachable. We'll stop, but we need to clear this like any other place."

"Agreed."

Kevin pulled into the gravel parking lot and turned off the engine.

Both men sat, looked and listened.

Nothing. No movement or sounds came from the house or surrounding area.

"I say we do this together. We'll go through the front door, but after we walk around the house first," Kevin said, getting out of the truck, his rifle firmly in his grasp.

"Okay," Paul said promptly.

With Kevin at point, they slowly walked around the right side of the house.

Kevin kept his eye on the windows, looking for any movement.

They entered the backyard to find a car parked near a wooden deck.

A clothesline spanned the distance of the small yard. Sheets and shirts flapped in the breeze.

Paul pointed to the clothes.

Kevin nodded. He swiftly but silently walked onto the deck and stopped just outside the back door.

Paul was right behind him, keeping his focus on anything behind them.

Kevin reached down and touched the knob, turned it, gave the door a slight push, and it opened. He peeked his head in and saw it led to a kitchen and beyond that a short hallway. A pungent rotting smell swept over him. He recoiled and jerked his head back.

The odor hit Paul's nostrils. He coughed and quickly put his left hand to his mouth to prevent from throwing up.

Kevin pulled a bandana from a cargo pocket and tied it around his face. He looked back to find Paul bent over. "Get it together."

"What's that smell?" Paul groaned.

"Rotting flesh," Kevin answered. "Now let's go clear the building."

Paul stepped away and moaned. "It's fine. I'll shit outside."

"Seriously?"

"I'm not going in there," Paul said, walking away.

"Where are you going?" Kevin asked.

"To see if there's napkins or something in the car to wipe with," Paul answered. He opened the car and rummaged through it. He popped his head back out and said, "Found some."

Kevin shook his head. Always curious but, more importantly, always in need of resources, he was going to suffer through the smell and scavenge what he could from the house. Before he stepped inside, he let his rifle hang from the two-point sling and removed his semiauto pistol. Giving one last look back, he saw Paul squatting on the far side of the car. He crossed the threshold and entered the kitchen.

The cabinet doors were closed, indicating the place hadn't been searched. He walked into the hall and discovered a bathroom on the right. He glanced in but saw nothing of importance. He moved past it into the living room. It had been converted into the showroom for the fabrics and quilts. Nothing there of interest either. To his right the stairwell headed up into darkness, but in front of him, to the right of the landing, was a closed door. He approached cautiously, his pistol at the ready. Using his left hand, he turned the knob and pushed the door open.

Flies swarmed out of the room and buzzed around him. The intensity of the smell grew, overwhelming his makeshift mask. He paused to overcome the urge to gag. The odor even affected his eyes as they watered.

In the corner, he spotted the source of the stench.

The body of a woman lay on a sofa, her hands perfectly folded on her chest and her eyes closed as if she were sleeping. Several empty prescription bottles sat on an end table. In the far corner, a man sat in a chair. What was left of his head hung down, resting on his chest.

It was evident she had overdosed while he had shot

himself.

Kevin marched farther into the room. He wanted to retrieve the weapon the man had used. As he drew closer, he spotted the body of a dog. It too lay as if it were sleeping. It was apparent they weren't going to let the dog go on living without them.

Kevin imagined scenes like this were probably commonplace across the country. The thought of people feeling so hopeless that they'd kill themselves made Kevin feel sorry for them. Since this had begun, he never once thought about taking his own life, even after Megan. Self-preservation ran deep in him. Yes, life sucked, but he'd rather be alive than dead.

He reached the desk and on the floor found a Smith and Wesson Model 19 .357 revolver. He picked it up, opened the cylinder, and saw there were five rounds still in it. He snapped it closed and shoved it into his waistband. On top of the desk he found a box of ammunition. He grabbed it and shoved it into a cargo pocket.

Knowing the man had that weapon, maybe he owned more. Kevin pushed the man's body aside and opened the drawers of the desk.

Nothing.

He spotted a small closet opposite the desk. He opened it and hit the jackpot. Standing right in front of him was an open gun safe full of numerous firearms, from long guns to handguns. The man had a small arsenal of weapons.

"Bingo!" Kevin said jubilantly. "Thank you, Paul, for

having to take a shit." Kevin filled his arms with an assortment of rifles and headed towards the truck. He exited the front door and rushed down the front steps.

"Kevin! Help!" Paul screamed from the backyard.

Not hesitating to respond, Kevin dropped the rifles and sprinted towards the back. He cleared the corner and ran full force into Paul, who was racing towards him.

Both men bounced off each other and fell to the ground.

Paul scrambled to his feet. He gave Kevin a bug-eyed look and cried, "A feral!"

Kevin looked up and saw the feral running at them. He raised his pistol, aimed as best he could, and let two rounds fly.

Both rounds missed. The feral seemingly anticipated the shots and leapt onto a chimney then climbed it to the roof of the house and out of sight.

"Shit!" Kevin barked. "Hurry, get to the truck!"

Paul didn't need instruction. He was already on his way.

Kevin followed.

A dark shadow cast down.

Kevin looked up and saw the feral hurtling through the air. Its target was Paul. With violent force, it slammed into Paul, causing him to smash against the grille of the truck. Instantly it began to swing its arms wildly, ripping and tearing at Paul's back.

Paul wailed in pain.

Kevin leveled the pistol and pulled the trigger repeatedly until the slide locked back. The numerous shots hit the feral in the back. It howled but kept swiping at Paul.

"Get it off meeeee!" Paul cried.

Kevin dropped the magazine and reached for another.

The feral's vicious attack slowed from the numerous gunshots it had received.

Paul shoved it off him and low crawled under the truck.

Kevin hit the slide release, leveled the pistol, and again pulled the trigger repeatedly.

The feral howled in pain.

"It hurts, doesn't it?" Kevin screamed at it.

The feral kept up its attack on Paul. He reached and took a hold of Paul's right leg and twisted.

Kevin heard a loud snap as Paul's leg broke.

Paul screamed then went silent.

The feral was not giving up its assault. It dug its nails into Paul's flesh and crawled up his leg towards his hips.

Kevin advanced, pointed the pistol at its head and hollered, "Die, motherfucker!" Then he pulled the trigger.

The shot was the last in the magazine and the one that finally put an end to the feral. With half its head gone, it went limp and toppled to the ground.

Not taking chances, Kevin reloaded and put one more bullet in its head for good measure.

***

Unable to travel until Paul's injuries were attended to,

Kevin took advantage of the house. He found a bedroom upstairs and began treating the multiple compound fractures and lacerations on Paul's back, buttocks and legs.

Groggy, Paul opened his eyes. He blinked repeatedly until the blurriness subsided. He saw Kevin standing over him and asked, "Am I dead?"

"If I'm what you see in Heaven, you're screwed, my friend," Kevin joked. His shadow danced on the far wall as a large candle flickered.

"The pain, it's so bad," he mumbled.

"I know. I haven't been able to give you anything. I've been waiting for you to wake up. You've been unconscious for twelve-plus hours," Kevin explained.

Paul looked to his right and watched the large flame. A tear streamed down the side of his face. "Am I going to die or, worse, turn into one of those things?"

"You're fine, no bites, nothing like that. I won't bullshit you though, your right leg is bad. I did my best to set it, but you have three compound fractures."

"This is it. I'm going to die," Paul cried, more tears flowing.

Kevin lowered his voice and said, "Calm down. I'll do anything to make that not happen."

"You promise?"

"Promise. Now if you can, I need you to take some ibuprofen. It's the best thing I have for pain management. I thought these people would have some good stuff but nothing. These must have been the healthiest people on the planet. I only found a bottle of Advil, a tube of

Preparation H and wart removal, oh, and a box of Band-Aids."

Paul held out his hand. "Give me, like, ten Advil."

"Let's start with six," Kevin said, pouring them into Paul's hand.

Paul tossed them back and drank the water offered him next.

"Now get some rest," Kevin said.

"The cuts and punctures, were you able to sew them up?" Paul asked.

"That I did accomplish. There was no shortage of thread and needles here," Kevin answered.

"Did any more of those things come?"

"No, by the way, where did it come from?" Kevin asked.

"In the far back, there was a Conex container; I went scavenging. I knocked on it, you know, expecting to hear something if one of those things was in there, but nothing. It was like it remained quiet on purpose. Anyway, I opened it up and it jumped out. I managed to hit it a couple of times. I ran, and next thing I know, I ran into you," Paul explained.

"Sneaky bastards, they're cunning. You can't treat them like simple dumb animals."

Paul grimaced in pain as he adjusted in the bed. "Dude, the pain is unbearable. My leg, it hurts so bad."

"I'll go looking for meds tomorrow. What I need you to do is try to get some rest, that will be your best medicine," Kevin said, exiting the room.

"Hey, Kev."

Turning around, Kevin said, "Yeah."

"Thank you for patching me up and for once more saving my life."

"You'd do the same for me."

"When you go looking for meds, look for another place too," Paul said.

"Why?"

"The smell, if my wounds don't kill me, that will," Paul joked, referencing the putrid odor that permeated the entire house.

CHAPTER ELEVEN

EAST OF TYHEE, IDAHO

JUNE 12, 2020

Kevin protested, but Paul insisted on going with him to find medicine. He was adamant that he wouldn't stay in the *stinking* house.

After using the full morning to load everything of value, they headed out.

Several miles away they found the road blocked by a jackknifed semi. Luckily, a side road was close by and headed north. At least they were still heading in the right direction.

The small county road was straight and clear, a positive for them, but soon they'd need to find fuel and real medicine for Paul.

Lost in thought, Kevin didn't notice Paul pointing.

"Food!" Paul cried out.

"Huh?" Kevin asked, looking around.

"Medicine, food, water!" Paul said, jabbing his finger in the air.

"What?" Kevin asked, looking around.

"Turn," Paul said, pointing behind them.

Kevin slowed the truck and looked at Paul. "What are you talking about?"

"Sign, a sign," Paul mumbled. Thick sweat was

beaded on his ashen forehead and cheeks. Dark circles under his eyes added to his distressed look.

"What sign?"

"There," Paul said, looking back.

Kevin put the truck in reverse.

"There!" Paul cried out.

Leaning against a post was a handwritten sign that read FOOD, WATER, MEDICINE, with an arrow pointing down the gravel road.

"How convenient is that," Kevin mocked.

"Go," Paul urged.

"You want me to follow a sign that probably leads to a trap?" Kevin asked suspiciously.

"GO!" Paul barked, pulling up his purple-colored swollen leg.

To Kevin, it appeared as if blood was pooling in the calf. If he didn't get proper care and antibiotics soon, he'd get sepsis.

"GO!" Paul blared as he shoved Kevin in a rare moment of anger, no doubt generated from the intense pain and vertigo he was experiencing.

"Fine, we'll go and check it out," Kevin said. He turned the wheel hard and sped off down the dirt road.

***

They encountered more signs. After the third one, a large farmhouse appeared on a ridge.

Kevin slowed and scanned the area.

Paul was lying down but sat up when the truck

stopped. "House, go!"

"I'm not going to just drive up without looking around. How do we know this isn't some sort of trap?"

Without notice, Paul vomited.

"Shit," Kevin muttered.

Paul was in bad shape and timing was everything.

Disregarding his normal procedures, he headed to the house.

As he approached, the house seemed abandoned like the last one.

Sitting behind the large two-story house with its wraparound covered porch was a large red barn and two smaller outbuildings. Stretching along the perimeter of the property was a white wooden fence.

Kevin didn't see any vehicles parked, but they could be out of sight behind the house.

Like before, he stopped at the front. He waited a few and got out, his rifle in hand like always. This time, he was going to take a different approach. "Hello!" he called out.

Paul opened his door and hollered, "Hello!"

No reply.

Kevin walked up the steps and onto the porch. With each footfall, his weight stressed the wooden deck, causing it to creak. He reached the front door and, as if he were a visitor, knocked.

"Hello!" Paul again hollered from the truck.

Kevin waited and knocked once more. With no answer, he tried the door. It was unlocked. He pushed it open and again called out, "Hello!"

Silence.

"Paul, sit tight. I'm going to check it out," Kevin said. He walked in and was instantly struck with the smell. This time it was pleasant; a sweet floral aroma filled the air. From the look of the furniture, the house was being maintained. He wiped his fingers on a small table in the foyer and looked at them. No dust. "Hello! My name is Kevin. I saw your signs along the road. I need medicine. Can you help me?"

Still no reply.

From room to room he went. No bodies, no carnage, no ferals, and no dust. The house was either perfectly preserved, which was impossible, or the occupants weren't home right now.

He cleared the house and discovered the signs weren't misleading. In the pantry, he found the shelves full of canned goods. Stacked on the back deck were rows of five-gallon jugs full of water, and in the mudroom, two tall cabinets were stocked with first aid supplies and bottle after bottle of prescription medication.

"Kevin!" Paul hollered.

Hearing Paul's plea, Kevin raced from the house to find Paul lying on the ground. His face was pale and sweat poured off him.

"My leg, it hurts, it hurts so bad," Paul cried.

Kevin picked him up off the ground and took him inside. He took him directly to the first bedroom he'd seen upstairs. "Here you go. I'll be right back." He hurried out of the room.

"Kevin, hurry."

"I will," Kevin said, not looking back. He bolted down the stairs, turned the corner to head towards the mudroom, and froze when he saw a young girl standing in the hallway. "Hi," Kevin said, a look of shock on his face.

"Why, hello," the girl said.

"I, um, I didn't just barge in. I called out, but no one answered. I, um, my friend, he's upstairs. He's badly injured. I need to get him some meds."

"Sure, you know where they are?" the girl said, stepping aside.

Kevin hesitated to move, as her demeanor seemed…odd. "Um, are your parents here?"

"Unfortunately, no. They're not," she replied, showing no emotion.

"Will they mind that we're here? We saw the signs on the road," Kevin said.

"Not at all, that's why we put them there. We welcome all. Please, go get what you need," she said, pointing towards the mudroom at the back of the house.

Paul's groans could be heard downstairs.

"That's your friend. Please, go get what you need," she urged.

"Ah, thank you," Kevin said, rushing by her. In the mudroom, he took what he needed: fresh bandages, suture kit, antiseptic, antibiotics, and some morphine in capsule form. He went to the kitchen, filled a large bowl with warm water, and nestled it in his arms.

Paul's groans grew louder.

Kevin exited the kitchen but stopped abruptly so as

not to walk into the girl. He looked at her and noticed something was different. Around her neck hung a small chalkboard and her black hair hung straight down, as opposed to being pulled back into the long ponytail she had been sporting moments before. "Excuse me."

Not saying a word, she sheepishly stepped out of his way.

Kevin marched upstairs, not giving any more thought to his encounter.

"Kevin," Paul moaned.

Rushing into the bedroom, Kevin said, "I'm here, buddy. Let's get your wound cleaned up and I've got some better drugs." He put everything on the nightstand and promptly popped the top of the morphine bottle open. Noticing he forgot a glass of drinking water, he jumped up and turned towards the door.

"I thought you might need this," the girl said, holding a glass of water.

Surprised to see her, he replied, "Oh, great. Um, thanks." He took the glass and gave it to Paul. "Drink and wash this down." He handed Paul a single capsule.

Paul happily took the morphine.

"Now, let's get your pants off so I can clean this wound," Kevin said just before stopping. He looked back to see if the girl was there; she wasn't, so he proceeded.

Paul was weak, barely able to put the glass on the nightstand. He winced in pain as he shifted in the bed. "Who was that?"

"She lives here," Kevin answered. When he saw Paul's swollen and deeply purple leg, he cleared his throat and said, "Blood is pooling. I'm going to have to open up the sutures and drain it."

"Whatever, do whatever, just make it right." Paul grimaced.

He shot Paul a look and said, "I'll do my best. I'm not a doctor. I barely know first aid."

Paul patted Kevin's arm and said, "I trust you."

***

Kevin closed the bedroom door and turned to find the girl standing near the top of the stairs. "Hi."

"Hello. How is your friend doing?" she asked.

"He's resting. We'll see how the meds work now," Kevin answered.

"Good. Are you hungry?" she asked.

"Ah, yeah, sure," Kevin answered. He was finding her welcoming demeanor a bit disarming, yet she seemed genuine.

"Good, 'cause I made lunch," she said. She turned and proceeded down the stairs.

Kevin took a few steps. He stopped at the first step and listened. *Is she talking to someone?*

Down below, the girl was talking in a conversational tone.

Kevin came down the stairs, careful not to spill the bloody water in the bowl. At the landing he turned and saw the girl. Again her hair was down and the chalkboard was around her neck. "Hi. You startled me."

She looked away and hurried towards the kitchen.

"Weird," Kevin said under his breath.

The girl disappeared into the kitchen.

Kevin was right behind her. The first thing he saw was the girl at the small dinette table. He headed to the sink and poured the water down the drain. Seeing a bar of soap, he grabbed it and washed his hands.

Whispering came from behind him.

Unnerved, he did an about-face and saw two girls. The girl with the chalkboard was sitting and the one with her hair pulled back into a ponytail was standing next to her. They were identical twins.

"Sit down. I made you a peanut butter and jelly sandwich," the girl with the ponytail said, pointing to the head of the table. "I hope you don't have peanut allergies."

"Now it makes sense. There's two of you." He chuckled. "I thought I was losing my mind for a second and, no, I don't have peanut allergies."

"Please, sit down, eat. You must be hungry," the girl standing said.

Kevin toweled his hands off and did as she suggested. Taking the sandwich in his hands, he marveled that the bread was moist. "I have to ask, where did you get the bread? It looks fresh."

"We made it."

"Your oven works?"

"Why, yes, everything works in this house. Why wouldn't it?"

"Because some of the power has been going out, yours still works?"

She walked over to the light switch and flipped it up. The overhead lights turned on. "Our power did stop, but we have solar. Daddy installed solar panels out past the barn."

"What will you do during the winter?" Kevin asked, taking a bite of his sandwich.

"Powerwall," she answered.

"What's a powerwall?"

"Daddy was an engineer for Tesla. On the back of the house, we have one installed with enough batteries to power the entire farm," she said.

Kevin sat back and cocked his head. *How is this girl so smart and articulate?*

"Do you want to see it?" she asked.

"After I eat," Kevin replied. He gave the sister a look. As she picked at her sandwich, she gave Kevin suspicious looks. "How old are you girls?"

"We're twelve," the girl standing said.

The other girl shook her head vigorously.

"Sorry, we're twelve and a half."

"I have to apologize. I'm sitting here eating your food and my friend is upstairs recuperating with medicine you provided, but I haven't introduced myself. My name is Kevin and my friend upstairs is Paul."

The girl standing smiled and said, "My name is Claire and my little sister here is Chloe."

Chloe shook her head and gave Claire a bad look.

"She hates it when I call her my little sister, but she is three minutes younger than me," Claire said with a devilish smile aimed at Chloe. "And that does technically make her my younger sister."

Chloe reached into her pocket, pulled out a piece of chalk and scribbled on the chalkboard.

Kevin watched curiously.

Finished, she held it up to Claire.

DON'T BE MEAN. I'LL TELL MOTHER, it read.

Kevin read it and immediately asked, "Where are your parents?"

"Daddy was killed and—" Claire said before being interrupted by Chloe grunting. "What? What am I supposed to say?"

"And your mother?" Kevin asked.

Claire leered at Chloe and replied, "She's gone."

"Gone like she'll be back soon?" Kevin asked.

Chloe shot up from her seat. She cut her eyes at Claire and marched off, fists clenched.

"She's upset. I'm sorry, the topic of your mother is a sensitive one?" Kevin asked.

Like flipping a switch, Claire brushed off the encounter with Chloe. She turned to Kevin and asked, "Are you thirsty? We have pop, or I can make some coffee."

"You have coffee?" Kevin asked, his eyes widening with joy. He remembered his comments just yesterday about it. "Coffee would be great."

CHAPTER TWELVE

THE FARM, EAST OF TYHEE, IDAHO

JUNE 13, 2020

The sun's early rays hit Kevin's face. Stretching, he opened his eyes and gazed out the double-hung window towards the rolling fields beyond. Thoughts of Megan came and how they had dreamed of owning a property like this.

With the sun hanging just above the horizon, it meant he'd slept in. *Is Paul doing okay?* The last time he'd seen him was the night before, and the medications had seemed to be doing the trick. He wanted nothing more than to lie in bed, but duty called. He sat up and again stretched. He swung his legs out and stood. Out of the corner of his eyes, he caught a glimpse of his physique in the mirror. He paused and looked. He'd leaned up since everything had happened. Never an overweight person, he always thought he could lose another ten. Well, he had achieved it, who knew that all he needed was a mutant apocalypse to get him to his ideal weight.

Laughter came from Paul's room.

Curious, Kevin quickly put on some clothes and headed there. He approached the doorway but stopped before walking in.

Paul made funny animal noises then laughed

heartedly. "Coming all the way from Asia is Randy the rhesus monkey," Paul said in a deep voice followed by hooting and squeaking calls.

Clapping sounded.

Kevin peeked his head in and saw Chloe sitting on a chair at the foot of the bed.

Paul was sitting up, making animated gestures.

"Good morning," Claire said behind Kevin.

Kevin jumped and turned. "You scared me. You're like a ninja, always sneaking up."

"Sorry, it wasn't my intention to startle you. Are you hungry?" Claire said.

"How long has Chloe been in there?" Kevin asked, ignoring her question about food.

"Long enough," Claire said, walking past Kevin and into the room. "Come, Chloe, Paul needs to rest and you have chores to do."

Chloe rolled her eyes and stood. Stomping her feet, she exited the room with Claire right behind her.

Claire stopped in front of Kevin and said, "Breakfast is on the table. I made muffins this morning."

"Muffins, wow," Kevin said. He patted his belly and thought that if he kept eating, his mutant apocalypse physique might turn into a dad bod.

"And there's fresh coffee too," she said, walking off.

With a big smile, Kevin walked into the room and said, "I feel like I'm at a bed and breakfast."

"They're nice," Paul said, a grin gracing his face too.

Kevin sat on the edge of the bed and asked, "How do you feel?"

"A bit better, my leg still hurts, but the morphine is helping, a lot."

"You look better," Kevin said. He pulled the sheet back and looked at Paul's leg. It was swollen but not as much as yesterday. "Leg looks good. Did you take your dose of antibiotics yet?"

Paul gave him a thumbs-up.

"Did she talk at all?" Kevin asked, referencing Chloe.

"Nope, only wrote on her little board."

"Hmm, she's not deaf, just mute. Odd. You know, I've never met a mute person before, I guess there's a first for everything."

"She can hear perfectly well. I asked her if they had any games and she wrote *yes*."

"Going to play some games, are you?" Kevin asked.

"I'm not going anywhere. Have to find some way to pass the time," Paul said.

"You do feel better. You have pep; you seem happy," Kevin said.

"I'm not a hundred percent, but this feels amazing compared to yesterday. So, yes, I am happy," Paul answered, his grin widening across his face.

"Good, let me go get some food. I'll bring you up some too," Kevin said, getting up.

"No need, Chloe brought me up a muffin; they're off the charts. Actually, if there are any more, grab me another."

"Your appetite is back, that's a good sign," Kevin said, walking away. He stepped into the hallway and closed the door behind him.

From downstairs, loud whispers came up the stairway.

Curious, Kevin approached the top of the stairs quietly and listened.

"I don't care...stop...stop writing...you know what Mother would say," Claire said. "Two days, no longer...now go back to your chores."

A loud crash sounded.

"You broke Mother's favorite vase!" Claire barked.

Kevin leaned closer to hear. His elbow hit two small framed pictures, causing one to fall off the wall. It hit the wood floor hard, shattering the glass.

Claire marched over to the landing and looked up. "Is everything okay?"

"Yes, sorry, I accidentally hit...I'm so sorry," he said, bending over and picking up the framed picture of the girls when they were younger.

"What broke?" Claire said, running up the stairs.

"A picture of you and Chloe," Kevin said, holding it up for her to see.

Claire took the picture out of his hand and looked at it. "Oh, that one. I always hated that one. Go down and get breakfast. I'll clean up."

"No, I'll do it. I made the mess," Kevin insisted.

"No, please go. This will take me just a second."

"You sure?"

"Yes," she said with a smile.

Kevin did as she asked. He made his way down the stairs and headed to the kitchen. Along the way he saw Chloe sweeping up the fragments of the vase.

She gave him a sour look.

He ignored her and went into the kitchen. The aroma of chocolate chip muffins filled the air, watering his mouth. On the counter, an old coffee percolator was bubbling. Chocolate chip muffins and hot coffee wasn't the breakfast of champions, but he didn't care about putting on the troublesome ten pounds. Life now was meant to be enjoyed and enjoy he would.

***

The late morning and early afternoon were spent playing board games. Kevin joined in. He decided he wasn't going to have Paul and Chloe having all the fun. The one noticeable person absent was Claire; she instead continued her chores around the house, inside and out.

Chloe scribbled on her board and held it up for them to see. It read *THIRSTY? POP?*

"Soda sounds great," Paul exclaimed.

"Sure, I'll have one," Kevin replied.

Chloe happily jumped up and ran out of the room.

"Yesterday she was dour; now she's happy, like you," Kevin said, picking up on Chloe's improved mood.

"Yeah, she's sweet. Claire, on the other hand, what a little bossy pants."

"Don't be hard on her. She's taken on the typical older sibling role. With both parents dead, she's stepped up. I admire her. Look at this place. She runs a tight ship. It's awesome," Kevin said.

"Maybe she's too strict."

"You're crazy. The world has fallen apart, but if you only saw this place, you'd think the world hasn't changed one bit. I don't know how they've managed so far, but it's quite impressive," Kevin said.

Chloe appeared in the doorway, holding three bottles of RC cola.

"I haven't had RC in…heck, I don't think I've ever had it," Kevin remarked, taking the chilled bottle.

Paul couldn't wait to get his hands on the ice-cold soda. He took it and immediately poured half the bottle down his throat.

"Easy," Kevin scolded.

Paul pulled the bottle away from his mouth, burped and said, "Sorry."

Chloe smiled and clapped.

"Where's Claire?" Kevin asked.

Chloe replied by simply shrugging her shoulders.

Kevin looked over his shoulder and out the window. The afternoon sun was still riding high. It was hours before sunset. He hadn't heard Claire moving around downstairs, so he decided to take a break and go look for her. "If you'll excuse me." He got up and left the room.

Downstairs, he couldn't find her. *Maybe she's outside?* He headed for the back door but stopped when he heard several loud bangs on the front door. He was close enough to see through the glass in the back door and spotted Claire exiting the barn. *Who could that be?* he suddenly thought.

"Maggie, Tom!" a female voice cried out.

The doorknob rattled but didn't open. Kevin had

seen to that by making sure he locked the doors.

"Maggie!" the woman called out.

Kevin ran back to the stairs. He wasn't sure who it was and had no intention of letting in someone who meant him harm. He reached the landing and heard a scream.

The woman was staring at him through the side window. "Who are you? Where's Tom and Maggie?"

Deliberately ignoring her, he raced up the stairs and to his room. He grabbed his pistol and headed to Paul's room.

"Hey, what's going on?" Paul asked from his room.

Kevin walked in. "Not sure, I think she knows them, but I'm not taking any chances," he said, holding his pistol firmly.

Chloe walked to a window that overlooked the front drive. She peered down for a second and came back. She wrote on her board and showed them. *MY AUNT TERRY. SHE'S FINE.*

Voices came from out front.

Kevin ran to the window and looked down to see Terry hugging Claire. Seeing the woman was a family member, his urgency melted away. He shoved the pistol into the small of his back and covered it with his untucked shirt.

Knocking from the front door.

"Open up. It's just Aunt Terry," Claire called out.

Kevin waved Chloe over and said, "I'll follow you down. I think it's important you open the door, not me, a stranger."

She nodded.

"Hurry up!" Claire yelled.

Chloe rushed down, unlocked the door and opened it fully.

Terry leapt across the threshold and snatched her in her arms. "Oh, I've missed you."

Chloe just stood, her arms plastered to her sides.

Tears flowed down Terry's cheeks. She pulled away and said, "Let me get a look at you. Oh, my sweet little girl, how I've missed you. Are you good, healthy? Claire, tell me, who is this man?"

"Visitors who arrived yesterday. His name is Kevin. His friend Paul is hurt. One of those monsters broke his leg," Claire replied.

"Have they hurt you, touched you in any way inappropriately?" she asked.

"Listen, we came here because we saw the signs posted along the road. My friend was attacked; he was hurt badly. We needed meds, that's all. We're not bad guys, just in need is all," Kevin said defensively.

"If you have what you need, then move on. This isn't your home," Terry barked.

"We will leave as soon as Paul is able. He's on the mend, but he needs a day or more."

Chloe chalked a note on her board and showed it to Terry. It read *THEY ARE NICE.*

"I'm sure they are, but this isn't their home and you're alone," Terry said.

Chloe looked at Claire and furrowed her brow.

"I told her both Daddy and Mother are gone," Claire

said directly to a clearly concerned Chloe.

"Chloe, honey, why are you writing on a chalkboard? Is something wrong with your throat?" Terry asked.

Kevin perked up; he too was curious about this.

Claire cleared her throat and replied, "After what happened to Daddy and Mother, she stopped talking."

"Oh, baby, I'm so sorry," Terry said, hugging Chloe once more. "I'm here now. I'll take care of you two."

"Anyone with you?" Kevin asked.

Terry gave him an odd look and answered, "Yes, I have a boyfriend coming soon. He could be here anytime."

"You came separately?" Kevin asked.

"Yes, I had my car and he had a truck. You know, with all our stuff," Terry replied.

"Um, okay, then I'll keep the gate open. Actually, I was thinking, Claire, I want to take those signs down. No need drawing attention to your place," Kevin said.

"I agree with him. What were you thinking? Why would you direct people to the house?"

"I thought we should help. Daddy always said we should help people. We have so much, we should share," Claire answered.

Terry glanced at Kevin, then put her gaze on Claire. "You need to take those down. Not everyone out there is nice, trust me. After driving all the way from Sandpoint, it's a tad bit different. If those things don't try to get you, bad people will try."

"Tell me about it," Kevin agreed.

"Let him—what's your name?"

"Kevin."

"Yes, let Kevin go out and gather those signs up. And let us go inside and catch up. I want to hear everything." She put her arms around both girls and walked them towards the living room.

Kevin closed the door and locked it. He turned back around and said, "I'm going to get some gear and head out to grab those signs. Please check on Paul while I'm gone."

"Okay," Claire hollered back.

He headed upstairs, got his stuff and headed back. On his way past Paul's room, he called out, "I'll be back shortly."

Paul replied, "Huh?"

At the bottom, he found Chloe standing there.

She held up her board. I'LL WATCH PAUL.

Kevin looked deeply into her green eyes. He saw tenderness, but also much pain. Like so many children who were still alive, they had suffered through a lot. He couldn't imagine being left or orphaned. The thought was heartbreaking. He bent down and softly said, "You're very nice. Thank you."

She nodded and ran upstairs.

CHAPTER THIRTEEN

THE FARM, EAST OF TYHEE, IDAHO

JUNE 14, 2020

A scream jolted Kevin awake. He dashed from his room, pistol in hand.

A second scream, this time more of a wail. It was coming from Paul's room.

He burst through the door to find Paul on the floor, covered in blood. He was grabbing at his broken leg. "You okay? What happened?"

"I slipped. I landed on my leg. I think I broke it again," Paul cried.

Kevin slid over and looked. He couldn't see anything that looked like a break, but two of the sutures were busted open. They clearly were the source of the blood.

"What's going on?" Terry asked, running into the room.

"I've got this. Go back to bed," Kevin ordered.

Claire and Chloe appeared in the door, but only stood watching.

Terry ran to Paul's side and began examining the leg. "Dear God, this is horrible. Who—"

"He'll be fine. He slipped and landed on it getting out of bed," Kevin said. He looked at Paul and continued, "And what were you doing getting out of bed?"

"I had to pee. The bed is so high, I slipped."

Kevin shoved his arms underneath Paul and lifted.

"Where are you putting him?" Terry asked.

"On the bed, I need to clean him up and re-suture the wounds."

"He's going to get the mattress soaked in blood. It will ruin it," she said.

Holding Paul, Kevin asked, "Then what should I do with him?"

"Put him back down on the floor. From the amount of blood coming from his leg, I have a distinct feeling his little mishap resulted in him cutting an artery."

"What?" Kevin asked, shocked.

"There's too much blood. It has to be that," Terry said confidently.

"You're just guessing, how would you know?" Kevin mocked.

"Because I'm a nurse practitioner. This sort of falls into my wheelhouse, as they say," Terry snarled.

"Oh."

"Kev, listen to her, please," Paul said.

Terry grabbed a pillow and put it on the wood floor. She stripped a blanket off the bed and laid it down. "Put him down, gently."

On the floor, Paul squirmed from the pain.

"I'm going to need you to go get some fresh bandages, warm water, hell, just bring up the entire trauma kit. I know they have one," Terry ordered.

Kevin ran out of the room with Claire just behind

him.

Chloe stood frozen, tears moistening her eyes.

Terry removed the bandages and began a careful examination.

Blood seeped from the broken sutures and his leg started to swell.

Out of breath, Kevin re-emerged holding a large blue trauma kit.

Claire came in next, holding a large bowl of warm water. "I got the water."

"Good," Terry said.

"Aunt Terry, we have a long folding table; would that be better than having him on the floor?" Claire asked.

"It would. Go get it. Kevin, go help," Terry ordered.

The two left and came back within minutes.

"Here," Kevin said, setting up the table.

Claire laid out a thick blanket on top.

Terry and Kevin picked Paul up and set him on top.

Paul groaned.

"Get me a belt, hurry," Terry said.

Kevin grabbed Paul's from the dresser and handed it to her.

Terry wrapped it around his thigh and cinched it down tight.

Paul cried out in pain.

The blood flow from his leg slowed.

Terry got up and motioned for Kevin to step aside with her.

Noticing this, Paul cried out, "What is it? What's

wrong?"

Terry whispered, "From my brief examination, I'm pretty sure one of the broken bones cut open an artery. He's bleeding out badly. I'm going to have to perform surgery just to examine where and to what extent the artery is damaged, that's not even getting into how badly the bones are broken or if they're even set right. I don't know what happened to him, but the damage to his leg is catastrophic under these conditions. Without the proper tools, etcetera, he probably won't be able to walk again, but that's if I can find the artery and sew it up. Also, his knee, did you see it? It's also suffered. It appears the breaks came from the leg being contorted or twisted."

"His knee is broken?"

"The cap is off center. What happened?"

"A feral grabbed his leg and, just as you guessed, twisted. The leg snapped like a twig."

"I'm right here, guys. What are you discussing? I have a right to know!" Paul yelled.

Ignoring Paul, Kevin asked, "I'm following your lead. What do we do?"

"I can't keep a tourniquet on it forever. I'm going to have to perform surgery to find the damaged artery and try to sew it up. If I fail, the only other option is to amputate the leg."

***

Kevin exited Paul's room, his clothes covered in blood. Tired and emotionally run-down, he sat on the top step and hung his head. The procedure had failed, but Terry had tried valiantly. That left them with only one option.

Terry followed. "I'm sorry. We're going to have to take the leg."

Kevin didn't reply.

She stood over him and said, "The sooner we get going, the better."

"How do we know he won't wake during the procedure?" Kevin asked, referring to the cocktail of drugs they had given Paul to make him unconscious.

"I don't, but the longer we sit around, the greater the chances are he'll wake."

"Can we give him more?" Kevin asked.

"I don't want to risk it," Terry said. Her face turned dour. "I'm truly sorry, I wish I could have done more. Two of the breaks have jagged edges, and the damage they've done to the artery and surrounding veins is too much, not to mention the calf is filling with blood. I either take the leg or we need to give him some blood, but we can't wait much longer, the loss of blood is putting stress on his organs."

"I'm coming, it's just that…I don't know how to put it."

"You've been a great help, thank you, but your friend needs just a bit more of your time."

Claire appeared on the landing below. "Can I help in any way?"

"No, dear, just stay downstairs. How's Chloe?"

"She's upset, but she'll be fine," Claire answered.

"We'll be done soon," Terry said.

"Okay," Claire said and walked off.

"They're good girls," Kevin said.

"They are. Now, let's finish this."

Kevin got up and walked into Paul's room. He looked at Paul lying unconscious. Thoughts began circulating on how he'd tell him his leg had been cut off. *How does one tell someone they had to cut their leg off?*

Terry quickly assembled all the items she was going to need.

Unsure of how to help, Kevin just stood by Paul and waited for orders. "Sorry, buddy," he said, patting Paul's arm.

Terry approached the table, inhaled deeply and asked, "Are you ready?"

Kevin sighed and answered, "As ready as I'll ever be."

Terry swabbed the area, took a scalpel and said, "Here we go." She made an incision all the way around the leg, cutting to the bone. With the flesh cut, she took hold of a hacksaw and slid it into the incision until it touched the bone.

Kevin's face turned ashen and he looked away.

"Don't give out on me now," Terry said.

"I'm fine," Kevin said.

"Good, now hold his leg steady. We're almost done," she said and began to saw the bone.

***

Unable to leave Paul's side, Kevin sat. He wanted to be

there the second Paul woke.

Chloe also felt compelled to wait. She relaxed in the far corner of the room, biding her time sketching on a pad.

Paul groaned.

Kevin's eyes widened. He leaned in close and patiently watched Paul wake.

Paul rolled his head from side to side, blinking heavily.

Chloe tapped Kevin on the shoulder.

Not hearing Chloe approach, Kevin looked shocked to see her standing next to him. "Gosh, you're so sleuth like."

She held up her chalkboard. *Is he awake?*

"I think so," Kevin replied.

"Kevin, what happened?" Paul mumbled in a groggy voice.

"Hey, buddy, how do you feel?" Kevin asked.

Paul adjusted in the bed, stopping when he felt a sharp pain shoot up from his leg. "Argh, my leg, it still hurts, real bad."

"Where?" Kevin asked.

"The calf, did she fix it?" Paul asked.

Confused, Kevin asked, "Your calf hurts?"

"Yeah. Did I mess it up more when I fell out of bed?" Paul asked.

"Um, yeah, you did. It appears two of the breaks cut through an artery, and the lower part was crushed so bad that the blood was filling up the leg. We operated—"

"You operated, really? I thought you all were just

talking big. She really operated on me?" Paul asked, grimacing as he tried to sit up.

"Just lie down. You need a lot of rest."

The door burst open, and Claire walked in. "I heard you all talking. Is Paul hungry? I just finished making dinner."

"He just woke, but he's in a lot of pain," Kevin said.

"I can eat something, for sure," Paul said.

Claire walked over to Paul and tenderly touched his shoulder. "I'm sure you must be hungry. I'm sorry about the pain."

"My leg is really hurting. I think I need some more painkillers," Paul said, referring to his now amputated leg.

"Your other leg hurts?" Claire asked, confused.

"No, my broken leg, it's in a lot of pain," Paul replied.

Claire gave him an odd look and turned to Kevin. "You didn't tell him?"

Chloe began to scribble on her chalkboard.

Wide-eyed, Kevin said, "How about we just let him rest." He cocked his head and gave Claire a look suggesting she be quiet.

"Tell me what?" Paul asked.

"Get some rest, you need it," Kevin said. He was unable to spit out the words that Paul's leg had been amputated.

"Oh," Claire said, looking surprised. She pursed her lips and gave Paul a look of sympathy. "Sorry." She turned and left.

"Kev, what's she talking about?" Paul asked.

Chloe held up her chalkboard. *THEY CUT OFF YOUR LEG. I'M SORRY.*

Not paying attention to Chloe, Kevin continued to lie. "Just rest. I'll go get some food."

Paul read the sign. His eyes bulged and nostrils flared. He tossed off the sheet and stared at the empty space where his lower leg used to be. "You cut off my leg!"

"We…um…listen, buddy, we had no choice. If we didn't, there was a high probability of you developing—"

"YOU CUT OFF MY LEG!" Paul bellowed, his face turning red with anger.

"We didn't have a choice," Kevin said defensively.

Tears burst from Paul's eyes as his composure changed to sorrow. "You cut off my leg," he whimpered.

"Paul, please understand, we didn't have a choice. It was that or you could die," Kevin said.

Chloe held up her sign, but no one read it.

Wiping the warm tears from his face, Paul cried, "I'll never walk, never run. I'm a fucking gimp. You should have just killed me."

"You're not a gimp, don't say that," Kevin said.

Chloe stepped in front of Kevin and shoved the chalkboard in Paul's face. It read *DON'T CRY. I'LL TAKE CARE OF YOU.*

With a shaky hand, Paul reached out and touched Chloe's arm. "Thank you. You're so sweet."

Embarrassed by the affection, Chloe looked down and blushed.

Paul looked up at Kevin and cut his eyes. "Get out!"

"Paul, please, don't be angry with me," Kevin said.

"GET OUT!"

Seeing he would be unable to console Paul, Kevin did just that. He left. In the hall he ran into Claire.

"I've got dinner for Paul." Claire smiled.

"Why?"

"Why, what?"

"You know."

"About his leg? He was going to find out sooner or later," Claire said. She walked around him and into the room.

***

Kevin entered the kitchen to find Terry eating.

"He knows?" Terry asked.

"Yeah," Kevin replied, walking to the stovetop to see what was for dinner.

"The chili is actually good," Terry said, scooping up a spoonful. "I'm not sure where these girls learned how to cook. My sister was horrible."

"Their dad?" Kevin said, ladling chili into a bowl.

"How did he take it?" Terry asked.

"Not good. You know something, Claire, she's smart, astute, but somehow couldn't pick up on cues that I wasn't ready to tell him. It was as if she was playing a devious game with me. Like she enjoyed the torment of Paul finding out and me not being able to tell him."

"She's just a kid, I'm not sure how well versed she is in cues," Terry said. "He knows and that's all that matters. I'm sure it was tough telling him."

"I didn't, Chloe did," Kevin replied.

Looking up from her bowl, Terry grinned and said, "She did?"

"I suppose those girls are tougher than I am. I was just having the most difficult time. How do you tell someone you cut off their leg?"

Shoving the empty bowl away from her, Terry answered, "Simple, just tell them. He was going to find out anyway."

"That's exactly what Claire said."

"She's a smart girl." Terry laughed. "Now let's discuss your staying here."

Peeking up from his bowl, he said, "Okay."

"Considering Paul's condition, you'll need to stay longer."

"You're not going to toss us out?"

"Not yet."

"Can I ask a personal question?" Kevin asked.

"Sure."

"Do you really have someone else coming to join you?"

Terry paused. "No. It's just me."

"I kinda knew, I just wanted to see how you'd reply."

"Can I ask a personal question?" Terry asked.

"Sure."

"What's your story? Where you guys heading?"

Kevin told her everything. From the first day until their arrival at the farm.

"They left you guys high and dry?" she asked,

referencing the others taking his truck.

"Yep. But I don't blame them. I don't think I would've done that, but I understand."

"And Paul was the reason for the breakup?"

"You could say that even in the apocalypse people can still be petty."

"I know that," she said, getting up and taking her bowl to the sink. She placed it in the basin and leaned against the bull-nosed granite edge. "It's getting dark."

"I saw your ring. Was your husband killed?" Kevin asked.

Claire crossed Terry's line of sight, headed for the barn.

"What's that?" she asked. Her thoughts had been on Claire and why she spent so much time in the barn.

"Your husband, is he dead?"

She turned around and answered, "Ha, no. What did you say, people are still petty? Well, Collin thought the end of the world was the best time to tell me he was leaving me to go be with his mistress. Can you believe it? Just when I need him, he ups and leaves me for some younger, hotter version." She looked at her ring. A scowl appeared on her face. Without further comment, she pulled the ring off and tossed it in the trash. "I was wearing it out of habit, but now that you brought it up, I don't need it anymore."

"Sorry about your husband."

"It just goes to show that you can't trust anyone."

"Agreed."

"Good talk. I'm going to go see if Claire needs any

help," Terry said and briskly exited the kitchen.

***

The early evening air felt good against her skin. She paused to take in the view to the west. Golden and orange hues streaked across the sky.

Her sister had always said the farm was where she'd die, and unfortunately it came to be. Those thoughts swiftly turned to regret. Countless times she had promised to come visit, but *more important* things always seem to find a way to prevent it. Now here she was, the only family the girls had. She wasn't the favorite aunt by any means, even though she was their only one. Her regret drifted to the girls and the reality that she hadn't fostered a relationship with them.

The clanking of metal tore her away from her thoughts. She looked towards the sound and saw Claire returning from the barn.

"What are you doing, Aunt Terry?" Claire asked, walking up quickly.

"I was coming to see what you were doing."

"Just preparing for dinner tomorrow," Claire said with a broad smile.

Terry leaned in and gasped, "Is that blood?"

Claire looked down at the dark stain on her shirt and quickly dismissed it. "It's nothing."

"It's blood. Are you hurt?" Terry asked, tugging at her shirt, attempting to lift it up.

Claire batted her away. "I'm fine. It's from the

chicken."

"Chicken?"

Reaching into the sack she was carrying over her shoulder, Claire pulled out a dead and headless chicken.

"Oh."

Claire stepped aside and said, "Want to help me pluck it?"

"You have chickens? What else do you have down there?" Terry said, taking a few steps towards the barn.

Claire froze and snapped, "Nothing. The chickens are around back in the henhouse. There's nothing in the barn except a tractor and all of Daddy's tools."

"Nothing fun to see or do? Like a big bale of hay to jump into from a loft?" Terry asked.

"Nothing fun like that. So, do you want to help me with the chicken?" Claire asked.

"I remember your mom telling me you had a horse or something. Where's that?"

"Dead."

"Oh."

"Aunt Terry, come, let's get this ready for tomorrow's dinner."

Terry stared at the barn. She'd been to the farm only three times in her life and had never stepped foot inside. For some reason she felt a strong urge to do so now. "Let me just look inside."

"Aunt Terry, please! It's getting dark and there's no lights in there," Claire snapped.

Startled by her response, Terry stopped and looked back at Claire. "You alright?"

"I want to do this with you. Mom and I used to do it together all the time and, well…" Claire said but stopped when she began to whimper.

Terry marched back and embraced her. "Okay, sweetheart, let's go inside and get this bird cleaned up."

CHAPTER FOURTEEN

THE FARM, EAST OF TYHEE, IDAHO

JUNE 15, 2020

Kevin yawned and stretched as he made the short walk to the bathroom, guided by the moon's light.

As he relieved himself, the craving for Claire's chocolate pudding came. The timing was odd, but who's to complain about timing when the thoughts of rich chocolate pudding was tugging. He finished up and rushed downstairs, being extra cautious not to wake anyone.

In the kitchen, he opened the refrigerator door and scanned the shelves.

Spotting it on the second shelf, he whispered, "Bingo." He pulled it out, grabbed a spoon and took a seat.

His mouth watered thinking about the creamy and smooth pudding touching his tongue. He ripped off the plastic wrap and dove in. The first spoonful was amazing; the second, just as good. He grunted and groaned as he ate.

Creaking came from the back deck.

He froze and listened.

More creaking.

Kevin placed the bowl and spoon down and stood

up. Fortunately, the moon's light was streaming through the back kitchen window, close to where the sound was coming from.

A shadow crossed the window.

That was enough for Kevin. Someone was there and he was unarmed. He remembered where the knives were and went for them.

The doorknob jiggled.

He grabbed the first one his hand touched, a cleaver.

A second shadow crossed the window, followed by unintelligible murmurs.

These weren't ferals, these were humans.

Breaking glass sounded from the front door, telling Kevin there were three or more and they had now made their move. He sprinted from the kitchen towards the front door, cleaver firmly in his grasp.

A hand fished around on the inside of the door, looking for the lock.

Kevin reached the door, lifted the cleaver high and came down with force. The blade severed the hand at the wrist.

The owner of the hand screamed.

Kevin turned around and yelled, "Terry, girls, someone is here. Go get my guns, hide!"

Bullets ripped through the front door, barely missing him.

Heavy footfalls came from above.

Terry called out, "Kevin, what's going on?"

"Intruders, they're trying to break in. Go to my room; take the girls. My guns are in there."

Offering no debate, Terry went and did as he said.

The back door exploded open and two men charged in, their guns blazing.

The stairway landing was only a few feet away. Kevin jumped onto it and raced upstairs to his room but found the door closed. He knocked and cried out, "It's Kevin. Open up."

"Kevin, what's happening?" Paul called out.

Ignoring Paul, Kevin banged on the door. "Open up. It's Kevin."

The door opened. It was Terry; the two girls were behind her.

"Hide in the bathroom," Kevin ordered.

Terry and the girls immediately went.

Kevin found his pistol and rifle. He went to the bathroom and handed the pistol to Terry. "Here. If anyone but me comes in here, point and pull the trigger."

Terry nodded.

Kevin shut the door and took up a kneeling position next to the open doorway of the bedroom. He leveled the rifle and pointed it at the top of the stairs.

"Kevin, what's going on?" Paul cried out.

"We have some visitors. I've got this," Kevin replied.

Cries of pain echoed from below. "The motherfucker cut my hand off."

"You're fine. Now let's go get that piece of shit," a gruff voice snapped.

Kevin thought about warning them, but quickly dashed the idea. These weren't nice people; they were here with bad intentions.

"I know there's some sweet pussy upstairs. Now come on out!" the gruff voice yelled.

Kevin flipped the selector switch to *SEMI* on his AR and waited.

"Come out, come out, wherever you are!" the man hollered as he stepped onto the last step.

The reticle of Kevin's optics rested on the man's chest. Kevin squeezed the trigger. A 5.56 round blasted out of the muzzle and struck the man in the solar plexus. He reeled and fell back onto the wooden stairs. Gravity did the rest as he tumbled to the landing.

"Shit, those sons of bitches killed Bobby!"

"Fuck this, I'm out of here," the one-handed man barked.

"Where you goin'?"

"I'm out of here. Bobby was wrong; those little girls are killers. I don't want any of it."

"They're just little girls!" the other man hollered.

Hearing the men blathering, Kevin made his move. At the top of the stairs he could see the dead man and another standing close by. He aimed and repeatedly pulled the trigger.

Two of the rounds struck the man. He raced off, but soon the effects of the wounds were too much. His legs buckled and he fell to the floor.

Kevin ran down the stairs, hurdled the dead man at the bottom and headed in the direction of the other. He found him crawling on the floor near the dining room. He walked up and said, "Hey."

The man didn't reply. He kept crawling.

Not one to taunt, Kevin pulled the trigger once more. This round took off the top of the man's head. Brain matter and blood splattered onto the far wall.

The roar of a truck engine sounded in the distance.

Kevin wasn't done. He flew out of the house and charged in the direction he'd heard the engine.

Lights appeared over the ridge.

At a full sprint, Kevin ran, paying no concern to being barefoot. He was a man on a mission. The gate slowed him down, but wasn't enough to stop him from getting in range.

The truck made a U-turn and sped off.

Kevin still had over twenty rounds and he meant to use them if necessary. He stopped, leveled the rifle and pulled the trigger until the bolt locked to the rear.

The truck swerved and struck a tree.

Out of ammunition but full of anger, Kevin marched towards the wrecked truck. There he found the one-handed man semiconscious. He opened the door, took the man by the collar and yanked him out.

"It wasn't my idea," the man pleaded.

All Kevin had was his rifle. He raised it high above his head.

"Mr. Matthews?" Claire asked.

Kevin froze. He turned to find Claire standing a few feet away, the cleaver in her hand. "Go back inside."

Claire ignored him and stepped towards Mr. Matthews, the one-handed man.

"It's not safe out here. Go back inside," Kevin urged.

"Claire, where are you?" Terry cried from the house.

"She's out here, near the road!" Kevin shouted.

Claire approached Mr. Matthews, stopping inches from him.

"It wasn't my idea, it was Bobby's. He said—"

Giving no warning, Claire swung the cleaver and struck Mr. Matthews in the side of the head, penetrating deep into his skull.

Mr. Matthews grunted and started to twitch.

Claire pulled at the cleaver, but it was stuck.

"Claire, stop. He's dead," Kevin said.

Not listening, Claire growled as she tried to remove the cleaver.

"That's enough," Kevin said, this time grabbing her by the shoulder.

She turned, smacked his arm and yelled, "Don't touch me!"

Kevin raised his arms and replied, "Okay, but I'm not here to hurt you."

Terry appeared and ran up to them. "Claire, are you okay?"

As if in a trance, Claire pulled at the cleaver.

Chloe soon came up and walked over to Claire, putting her hand on hers. That was enough for Claire to stop. She let go, looked at Chloe and said, "He's dead."

Chloe replied by embracing Claire.

Kevin and Terry watched the two hold each other for what seemed like minutes.

Kevin, a man who had seen a lot since the outbreak, had never witnessed anything like what he'd seen Claire do, and doubted he'd see it again.

***

"Tell me everything that happened," Terry said.

"I can say it another way, but still it's as simple as she walked up, cleaver in hand, and hit him with it," Kevin replied.

Terry put her head in her hands and sighed loudly.

"I've never seen a kid do that, but then again, as of weeks ago I never imagined the world would end in a zombie apocalypse."

Chloe walked into the kitchen and held up her chalkboard. *SHE'S SLEEPING NOW.*

"Thanks for letting us know. Now it's time for you to go to bed too," Terry said, rubbing Chloe's arm.

Chloe turned and left.

"I'm going to take them," Terry blurted out.

"Where?" Kevin asked.

"Back home to Sandpoint. My community, we're on an island. We're safe there. We have security, walls. They can live without fear of those things or scumbags like those guys," Terry replied.

"That's a long drive. It's dangerous out there. Just stay here. We can build a wall around this place," Kevin offered.

"This place can never be truly protected. It's a nice place, big house, outbuildings, power, food, water—you name it, they have it here—but they can't keep it safe. Eventually someone will get in."

"Not if I'm here," Kevin said, reaching his hand out and touching hers.

She recoiled from his touch. "I just met you two days ago. I don't know you, and I've heard men boast about being there for the tough times. People lie, period."

Kevin bit his tongue. There was no way to convince her about his sincerity.

"I'm going to bed. In the morning I'll gather the girls and tell them. We leave tomorrow night at the earliest," Terry said.

"I'd suggest leaving first thing in the morning the following day, better to drive during the daylight hours," Kevin advised.

She nodded. "Good advice." She turned and headed towards the door.

"She knew him," Kevin said.

Terry stopped, faced Kevin and asked, "Knew who?"

"That man, she knew him. She called him by his name before planting that cleaver in his head. What do you make of that?"

"Apparently we have a lot to talk about tomorrow," Terry said and exited.

Kevin again silenced himself. He'd process what to say and deliver it tomorrow just before she was going to tell the girls. He turned off the light, walked into the darkened living room and lay on the couch, pistol in hand.

CHAPTER FIFTEEN

THE FARM, EAST OF TYHEE, IDAHO

JUNE 16, 2020

"Do you have any threes?" Paul asked, holding a handful of cards.

Chloe shook her head and raised her chalkboard. *GO FISH*. She turned it around, wrote something and held it up. *SEVENS?*

"Yep," Paul answered, removing a card from his hand and handing it to her.

A smile cracked Chloe's tender face. She wiped the board quickly with her hand and wrote *JACKS?*

"Is there a mirror behind me? Can you see my cards?" Paul joked, handing her the jack of clubs.

Chloe giggled.

A look of shock washed across Paul's face and his brow furrowed. "Did you just laugh out loud?"

Chloe looked down. Her dark straight hair fell around the cards.

"It's okay, your secret is safe with me," Paul said.

She slowly lifted her head and peeked at him between the draping strands of hair.

"I promise I won't say a word to anyone," Paul said, motioning with his hand over his heart.

She gave him a slight smile.

Wishing to move past the moment, Paul asked, "Is it my turn or yours?"

Chloe wrote on her board and lifted it up. *THANK YOU.*

"Of course, that's what friends are for," Paul said, smiling.

A knock at the door.

"Come in," Paul called out.

The door opened. Terry was standing there. "Chloe, come with me. I need to talk to you and Claire."

***

Kevin hammered the last nail into a small board that covered the broken window on the front door. He stepped back and admired his work. "Not pretty, but it will do the job."

"Have you seen Claire?" Terry asked.

"Last I saw her, she was heading to the barn," Kevin replied. "What's up?"

"I'm having that conversation with them," Terry answered. Just behind her stood Chloe, her arms dangling by her sides.

"Is there any way I can get you to reconsider your departure time? I ask because Paul and I can accompany you to Sandpoint."

"Paul won't be ready to travel long distance for a while."

"Why?"

"I told you why," Terry snarled.

"The *Paul can't travel* story is BS. What's the real reason?"

Chloe put her gaze on Kevin.

He looked into her eyes and felt unsettled. "How about we discuss this later?"

"Doesn't matter when we talk, the answer will be no. Look, feel free to set up shop here. This place is yours. This is an opportunity, not a setback."

Kevin thought. She was right in many ways. The house, the farm, it was stocked; they had power. This was perfect. Of course, they'd have to beef up security, but this place could work.

Chloe pulled on Terry's arm and pointed out the window.

Terry looked and saw Claire walking the perimeter, pushing a wheelbarrow. "What's she doing?" Curious, Terry went outside with Kevin right behind her.

"Claire, what are you doing?" Terry asked, walking up to her.

Holding a shovel in her small hands, Claire scooped up something from the wheelbarrow and sprinkled it along the fence perimeter. "It keeps the ferals out."

The pungent odor hit Terry and Kevin.

"Smells like shit, literally!" Kevin howled, covering his face with his arm.

Terry did the same but peeked into the wheelbarrow to inspect the contents. "What is it?"

"A compost I make using old horse manure and chicken poop. Daddy taught us," she replied, scooping up another shovel full.

"That smells God-awful." Terry gagged.

"Then leave me alone," Claire said smugly.

"I need to talk to you," Terry said.

Claire stopped and looked around. "It's nice here, isn't it? Mother always used to say that the sky was bluer here than anywhere else."

"When will you be done?" Terry asked.

Taking another shovel full, Claire answered, "A couple of hours."

Frustrated, Terry said, "I don't have a couple of hours."

Claire sprinkled the compost and asked, "What's the hurry?" She looked over her shoulder at Kevin and said, "Thank you for cleaning everything up." A reference to the bodies and mess made from the intrusion.

"Of course," Kevin replied.

Claire picked up the wheelbarrow and pushed it a few feet.

Finally answering Claire's previous question, Terry replied, "We're leaving. You, me, and Chloe. We're going north to Sandpoint. I have a nice house and we'll be safe there."

Claire stopped, turned and snarled, "We're not going anywhere. This is our home."

"No, it's too dangerous. You need to come with me," Terry insisted.

Claire looked at Chloe, who was standing a few feet behind Kevin. "Me and my sister aren't leaving with you or anyone. This is our home and you can't make us leave." She picked up her shovel and tossed a load of compost on the next spot.

"This isn't a debate. I'm your guardian now. You're coming with me," Terry snapped.

Claire threw the shovel on the ground, turned and faced Terry. "You're not our guardian, you're nothing. How many times did you come visit us? Never. Mother would ask and you always had something else going on. You were too busy or felt too important to give us the time of day. Suddenly you care? Just because you feel guilty for being a horrible person doesn't give you the right to come down here and take us away from our home, from Mother."

Chloe rushed to Claire's side and put her arm around her.

Kevin thought for a second and asked, "What do you mean by taking you away from Mother?"

"She's here, like Daddy. I won't leave them," Claire replied.

"Oh, sweetheart, I understand you don't want to leave the only home you know and the graves of your parents, but they're dead now. They'd want you to come with us. I know your mother would," Terry said softly.

Claire stormed up to Terry, looked up into her eyes and snarled, "We're not going anywhere."

"I'm sorry, but you are," Terry said. "We leave tomorrow, first thing."

"You can go, but we're not leaving," Claire said and marched off with Chloe tagging closely behind.

Kevin shook his head and said, "That didn't go over well."

"No, it didn't, but she needs to understand they don't have a choice. It's not safe here," Terry said.

Kevin thought about everything and offered his sincere opinion. "I'd suggest not forcing them. They've already been through a lot, and I have to admit, they seem to have a grip on things."

"Really? Like if those men broke in and we weren't here, you honestly think they would have been able to defend themselves? Please spare me your thoughts on how strong and capable you think they are," Terry snapped before heading off to walk the property.

"Where are you going?" Kevin asked.

"I need to think, I'm going to walk for a bit. I don't think it's a good idea to go back home just yet," she replied.

"By yourself? I don't think that's safe," Kevin said.

"I'll be fine," Terry said and walked off.

***

Kevin walked into the house and heard laughter upstairs. No doubt it was Paul being silly with Chloe.

The sound of pots and pans came from the kitchen.

He made his way there to find Claire preparing dinner with no real concern for how loud she was being.

"Chicken?" he asked, pointing to the plucked chicken sitting in a colander.

Claire didn't bother to turn around and look, she simply replied, "Yes."

"Hey, I don't know the entire family dynamic, but I do know—"

"No, you don't, you don't know anything," Claire interrupted.

"If you'll let me finish, I think you should listen to your aunt. At least hear her argument without rushing to a decision. Now, it sounds like she wasn't the best aunt, but I've lived long enough to know there's always two sides to a story. Just talk to her, ask why she wasn't around. You just might find something out about her that you never knew," Kevin said.

Showing her anger was still front and center, Claire grabbed the chicken and slammed it into the roaster and tossed in freshly cut potatoes. "Mother needed her and she was never available. Something always came up, especially men."

"I'm sure she and her husband had good reasons for cancelling trips down here," Kevin said, leaning against the doorjamb.

"Husband? Aunt Terry wasn't married, at least not in the normal sense," Claire blurted out.

Finding that statement unusual but not wanting to dive into it, he kept pressing for her to talk to Terry. "No one is perfect, you'll soon discover that when you get older."

"Daddy was perfect," Claire said just above a whisper.

Kevin heard her whisper and smiled. The daddy-daughter relationship was special, and hopefully he'd have that one day.

Claire looked up and saw Terry in the backyard, heading towards the barn. She quickly turned around and said, "You're right. I'll go talk to her. Why don't you go upstairs, get some sleep; you look tired."

"What?" Kevin asked, confused by Claire's sudden shift and urgency for him to leave. "You're going to talk to her?"

"Yes. You're right. I need to hear her side of the story, like you said."

"What about dinner?" Kevin said, pointing at the chicken.

She looked over her shoulder and said, "I'll take care of that after. I just saw her in the back; I'll go to her now."

Kevin felt a tap on his back. He turned to find Chloe holding her board for him to read.

PAUL WANTS YOU.

"I'll come right up," Kevin said and walked away.

The two girls looked at each other intently before Chloe followed Kevin while Claire went outside.

***

"Aunt Terry, hold up!" Claire hollered.

Terry stopped and turned.

Claire ran up and said, "Let's talk."

Taking a deep breath, Terry hesitated from her normal pushy self and asked, "What would you like to talk about?"

"Leaving."

"I'm pretty firm. While this farm is ideal in so many ways, it's not safe. My house, Sandpoint, is very safe. We have built a wall. Kids are going to school. We've fashioned a safe little town. You'll like it," Terry said.

"Do we have to rush away? I need time to process, but Chloe especially, she doesn't do well with sudden changes, at least not since…"

Terry waited for her to continue, but she didn't. Claire lowered her head and said, "You're probably scared of me after what I did to that man last night."

"Kevin said you knew him."

Claire didn't answer, she just held her head down.

Terry gently lifted Claire's head, looked into her eyes and asked, "Who was he?"

"A bad man."

"Who was he?"

"A neighbor, he lived on a farm over there," Claire replied, pointing off into the distance.

Terry looked in the direction she was pointing and asked, "Did they hurt you?"

Claire lowered her arm and replied, "I don't want to talk about it anymore."

"He did, didn't he?" Terry asked.

"I don't want to talk about it."

"That's exactly why I want to, scratch that, need to take you away. It's not safe here."

Claire's composure changed. She stared hard at Terry and exclaimed, "We're not leaving our home, EVER!"

"Claire, you need to understand that this is what your mother would want," Terry insisted.

"No, it's not!"

"I knew her better than you think. She wouldn't want you and Chloe alone out in the middle of nowhere, fending for yourselves."

"She would not!" Claire barked.

"Stop yelling at me. You and Chloe are coming with me. We leave tomorrow. I'm not debating this anymore. I'll drag you out of here."

"I'M NOT LEAVING, I'M NOT LEAVING, I'M NOT LEAVING, I'M NAAA…" Claire screamed.

Terry grabbed her arm and shook hard. "Enough!"

Loud clanging came from inside the barn.

Terry jumped. "What was that?"

"It's nothing, probably an animal," Claire said calmly, her demeanor making a drastic shift.

More clanging.

"Go back to the house and get Kevin," Terry said, pulling a small knife from her pocket.

"It's probably just one of the chickens. Come, let me show you," Claire said, walking to the barn door.

"Claire, don't," Terry warned.

Not listening, Claire opened the door and stepped inside, disappearing into the darkness.

Shocked and scared, Terry nervously approached the door.

Claire stuck her head out and said, "Come on inside. I know what the sound was."

Terry stepped over the threshold and into the pitch black.

Out of the corner of her eye, Claire spotted Chloe

standing in front of the large second-story hall window, gazing down. Claire nodded to her, turned around and said, "Over in the corner, Aunt Terry."

"I can't see anything. Turn on a light," Terry complained as she fumbled her way through the dark.

"Keep going, just a bit farther," Claire said as she closed the door.

***

Kevin rubbed the sleep from his eyes. From the kitchen, he heard the distinct sounds of chopping, and the smells that filled the room told him the chicken was roasting nicely in the oven.

He sat up and stretched. He hadn't planned on taking a nap, but after checking on Paul, he came back down and decided he'd do a little reading. It had only taken minutes for the heavy weight of fatigue to overcome him.

Chloe whizzed past and ran upstairs.

Kevin stood, turned and almost walked into Claire, who was standing but feet from him. "Good God, you startled me. How is it you can move around so quietly?"

She shrugged her shoulders and said, "I walk around normally. Maybe you need to get your hearing checked."

The last light of day shot through the window.

"How long was I asleep?" he asked.

"A few hours. You needed it," Claire replied. "Dinner is ready, come."

With each step he took, the savory aroma grew in

intensity, causing his mouth to water. "Wow, that smells amazing."

"Sit," she said and went to the counter. "White or dark?"

"A bit of both," he answered.

She prepared him a plate and put it in front of him.

His eyes grew with excitement as he stared down at the moist chicken and golden-brown potatoes surrounded by chunks of garlic and onion. He didn't wait; he picked up his fork and dove in. When the first forkful hit his mouth, he gushed, "This is so good. How do you know how to cook at so young?"

Standing proudly, she answered, "Mother, she taught me many things."

He put his fork down and gave her a sympathetic look. "I really am sorry you lost your parents. I can't imagine how hard it must have been to see them pass."

"It was harder for Chloe," Claire said.

"And that's why she doesn't talk?" he asked.

Claire paused. She looked down for a brief moment and said, "I made some iced tea, do you want some?"

"Yeah, sure."

Claire rushed to the refrigerator and pulled out a pitcher.

"How did the conversation go with Terry?" Kevin asked.

"Good."

"And?"

She put a tall glass next to him and said, "And what?"

"Was a decision made?"

"I told her we weren't going. She seemed fine with that."

"Just like that? She said she was fine with staying?" Kevin asked, surprised.

"I think she finally saw I was serious about not leaving."

Kevin looked around and asked, "Where is Terry?"

"I think she's upstairs. Maybe she went to bed early. She said something about being tired," Claire said, walking back to the refrigerator.

Kevin thought about her answer. It seemed odd to him she was fine with not going and now she was fast asleep.

"Speaking of being tired, I'm exhausted. When you're done, just put your dirty dishes in the sink. I'll clean them in the morning," Claire said and quickly walked off.

"Good night," Kevin said. He put his full attention back to his plate and proceeded to devour his food.

***

Whispers came from down the hall.

"Who's that?" Kevin asked, clearing the stairs. He tried to make out who it was, but the hall was dark.

A light appeared from the last room as the door opened.

Able to see, Kevin watched Claire and Chloe disappear into their bedroom and close the door behind them. Curious as to what they were whispering about, he went to their door and knocked.

The door opened almost immediately. "Yes," Claire said.

Kevin looked at her then to Chloe, who lay in bed. "Everything fine?"

"Yes. Why do you ask?"

"You both were creeping in the dark hallway," he replied.

"All good. Goodnight," she said and closed the door.

Kevin went from their door to Terry's. He stopped and thought about knocking, but if she was getting much-needed sleep, the last thing he wanted to do was wake her. He went from there to Paul's room. He knocked, opened the door and stuck his head in. "Hey, buddy."

"What?" Paul groaned, his focus on a book he was reading.

Kevin came into the room, pulled up a chair and asked, "How you doing?"

"Fine."

"Hey, did Terry stop by and check on your bandages?" Kevin asked.

"No."

"I would've thought she would."

"Why would she? You changed them earlier."

"Yeah, but I never told her I did. I just assumed she would have come and made sure you were fine, you know, healing nicely. She's a nurse, so I just thought she'd do some nurse-type stuff."

"Nope. Never saw her."

"You never saw her at all?"

"She didn't come see me, so, no, I didn't," Paul replied, his head still in his book.

"Did you see her walk by your room?" Kevin asked.

Irritated, Paul put the book down and griped, "Dude, enough of the twenty questions. I didn't see your girlfriend. She didn't come to my room, and I don't remember seeing her walk past my room. Next time I need to be on Terry duty, let me know."

"Easy. I just thought…you know, never mind. Have a good night."

"Yeah, yeah," Paul said. His contempt for Kevin was still strong.

Kevin left the room, closing the door behind him. He gazed over at Terry's door. *Should I knock?* Deciding again not to wake her, he headed downstairs to ensure the house was secure for the evening.

CHAPTER SIXTEEN

THE FARM, EAST OF TYHEE, IDAHO

JUNE 17, 2020

Kevin woke the second the sun's morning rays made their appearance over the rolling hills to the east. He first went to the kitchen but found it empty. Immediately, he dashed upstairs. There he found all the bedroom doors closed. It was early but not so early for *everyone* to still be asleep.

He opened Paul's door and peeked in to find him asleep and snoring. From there he went to Terry's; he leaned in and listened. Quiet. *Should I open it?*

"What are you doing?" Claire asked.

He turned and saw her standing feet from him. "Seriously? How do you not make any noise when you walk?"

Chloe rushed by him, her hair hanging in her face. Without a wave or anything, she hurried past and down the stairs.

"Hi, um, bye," Kevin said after Chloe.

"She's upset," Claire said.

"About what?" Kevin asked.

"Aunt Terry is gone."

Taken aback by what she said, Kevin turned and opened the door. The room was empty. "Where is she?"

"I don't know. I got up early, before the sunrise, and wanted to talk to her about our conversation yesterday. I went into her room and found she wasn't there. I went downstairs and looked around, nothing. By the way, you snore really loud. I think you might have sleep apnea."

"Huh, sleep apnea? No. Um, you came downstairs?"

"Yes. I even looked outside. She's nowhere to be found. Her car is still here," Claire said.

"Did she ever come back last night?" Kevin asked.

"I think so. Maybe she got up early or something. Went for a walk."

"You said she came in," Kevin snapped, his temper beginning to flare.

"I said I thought she was upstairs. After we talked, I came in. She was still outside. She said something about taking a walk," Claire countered.

Kevin was done talking. He took off and sprinted down the stairs. On the way past the couch, he grabbed his pistol and rifle and headed to the back door. Passing through the kitchen, he saw Chloe preparing a tray, no doubt for Paul. "Did you see Terry last night?"

A look of fear overcame Chloe. She looked down timidly and shook her head.

"Did you see her at all after Claire spoke with her?"

Chloe shook her head.

Kevin walked up to her and lowered his tone. "Look at me."

Chloe lifted her head and stared at Kevin.

"Why are you upset?"

Not wanting to answer, Chloe lowered her head.

"You're upset. Do you know something?"

"Leave her alone. She's merely upset after I told her that Aunt Terry is gone."

"Why?"

"Because she's her aunt, that's why," Claire snarled.

"Something happened to her, and I'm going to find out," Kevin said, marching off. He went past Claire and exited out the back.

Claire ran to the window to see where he was going.

Chloe tossed a few more items on the tray and hurried off towards Paul's room.

***

"Terry! Terry!" Kevin hollered, unconcerned if he was drawing attention to himself or the farm. Deep down he felt something bad at happened to her. He ran to the far fence line and yelled, "Terry! Terry!"

The sound of metal clanging came from inside the barn.

Kevin craned his head and looked. "Terry!"

The clanging turned to a loud banging of metal on metal.

"Terry?" Kevin asked as he approached the barn.

"Kevin, where are you going?" Claire called out, running towards him.

"Something is in there," Kevin said, waving her off.

"It's nothing," Claire said, getting in front of him, blocking his approach.

"No, it is something," Kevin said, gently pushing her

aside.

A strong wind swept in from the north and brought the smell of rotting flesh.

Kevin gagged and almost retched.

"It's probably the chickens. They get worked up," Claire said, running up and getting in front of him again.

Kevin looked down at her and asked, "What's that smell?"

"Nothing."

"Claire, what's going on?"

"Nothing!"

Kevin came around the back. The odor grew stronger with each step he took. A wood-sided enclosure draped with a blue tarp stood a few feet from the back side of the barn. The chicken coop sat just beyond that.

Whatever the smell was, it was coming from underneath the tarp.

He cautiously approached. He knew that smell, he'd come across it more times than he could remember.

"It's just the chicken droppings mixed with old horse manure," Claire said.

Kevin ignored her. He reached for the tarp but hesitated from lifting it. *Do I really need to see what's in here?*

"We should be looking for Aunt Terry," Claire urged, her tone shifting to one of concern.

Unable to restrain himself, he lifted one corner of the tarp. A swarm of black flies flew out followed by the strongest and most disgusting smells he'd ever encountered. He gagged and dry heaved a couple of times before gathering his composure. He looked inside and instantly recoiled at what he saw. He stepped backwards, looked at Claire and asked, "What, ah, what is going on here?"

She held out her hands, motioning for him to calm down. "Please let me explain."

Loud bangs came from the barn.

"What are...what have you...no, this is too much. Did you, no, you couldn't, did you?" Kevin stuttered as he stepped away from her.

"Let me tell you. Please let me explain," Claire said.

"Get away from me," Kevin said, pointing his rifle at her.

"Please don't shoot me. My sister needs me," Claire pleaded.

He jabbed a finger at the compost pit and asked, "Does she know?"

She took a few steps towards him and said, "If you just let me explain."

"Don't step any closer," he warned.

"You wouldn't shoot a child, would you?" she asked, taking another step.

"I know. I know what we'll do. We'll leave. We're leaving," he said, turning and running off towards the house.

***

Kevin burst through the back door. "Paul! Paul! We're getting out of here!" He sprinted to the stairs and ran up, skipping several at a time.

Alarmed, Chloe came from Paul's room, her dress smeared with blood.

Seeing her, Kevin screamed, "What have you done?"

Chloe gave him an odd look.

He shoved her hard against the doorjamb.

She smacked her head and fell to the floor.

Kevin came into the room, expecting to find Paul dead, but he wasn't.

"Dude, what the hell is wrong with you?" Paul shouted.

"You're alive. I thought when I saw her, I thought…"

"You thought she killed me? Dude, Chloe is a sweetheart. She changed my bandages is all," Paul replied, his face showing disdain mixed with surprise.

"Yes, I thought she killed you."

"Why the hell would you think that?" Paul asked.

"I'll explain later. We have to leave, NOW!" Kevin barked, tossing off Paul's sheet and leaning down to pick him up.

Paul pushed him away. "What are you doing?"

"We have to leave. There's no time," Kevin warned.

Paul had never seen Kevin act so terrified before.

"I'm going to say it slowly so you'll understand. We need to leave. The girls are dangerous. There's something in the barn. They—" Kevin said before being interrupted by Paul.

"Claire?" Paul asked, seeing her walk in.

Kevin spun around.

Claire held the cleaver tightly in her grip. She swung

hard and planted it in Kevin's forehead.

The blow to his head sent Kevin backwards onto the bed and on top of a frightened Paul.

Paul cried out in terror.

Claire stepped forward, grabbed the handle of the cleaver and pulled hard. The cleaver was buried deep like it had been in Mr. Matthews, but this time it came out.

Kevin was still alive. He mumbled something unintelligible as blood poured from the deep gash in his forehead and down his face.

Armed with the cleaver, she hit him again, this time striking Kevin in the face.

Kevin's body flinched and rolled off the bed, smacking the hardwood floor with a loud thump.

Paul continued to scream at the grisly scene playing out.

Claire pulled the cleaver from Kevin's face, turned to Paul, and lifted her arm.

Chloe appeared and grabbed Claire's arm. She shook her head and grunted.

"He knows," Claire seethed.

Chloe grunted and held Claire's arm tight.

"Let go!" Claire ordered.

Mustering all the strength she could, Chloe yelled, "NO!"

Claire couldn't believe her ears. She relaxed, lowered her arm and embraced Chloe. "You talked. You finally talked."

Seeing a chance to leave, Paul jumped from the bed, landing on his good leg, and started to hop away.

Chloe pulled away from Claire and put herself in between Paul and the door. She held out her arms and shook her head, signaling to him that he wasn't allowed to leave.

"Get out of my way," Paul pleaded.

Chloe wouldn't budge. She stood her ground, arms outstretched.

Claire walked over and said, "Chloe wants you to stay, so you'll remain our guest." She gave him a smile and took him by the arm.

Paul pulled away his trembling arm and cried, "Why?"

"Because you make her happy. Go back to bed…now," Claire ordered.

Petrified, he turned back and went to the bed, avoiding the pooling blood on the floor. He climbed in and pulled up the sheet.

Chloe rushed to his side, grabbed her board and wrote. *PLAY A GAME?*

"Play a game? My friend is on the floor, dead, killed by your sister, and you want to know if I want to play a fucking game?"

Stung by his response, tears welled in her eyes.

"Come, Chloe, let's give him some space," Claire said.

Chloe got up and walked out of the room.

Ensuring her sister was gone, Claire turned to Paul and said, "If you hurt my sister's feelings again, I'll kill you."

***

Paul fought the urge to sleep. He'd nod off for a second, but visions of waking up with a cleaver imbedded in his skull was his motivator to wake himself back up.

Throughout the day, Chloe kept checking on him, but he rebuffed her each time.

Claire returned twice. Once to remove Kevin's body and the second time to clean up the blood. Each time she remained quiet, never speaking a word but occasionally giving him a stern look.

Paul was beyond terrified, if that was even possible. It was one thing to see adults act savagely, or ferals rip and tear at their victims; it was another to witness a young girl brutally murder your only friend. His mind searched for an answer, a solution, but none came without him having to confront Claire. Escape was the only way he'd survive, but that required moving, and that was something he was having a difficult time doing considering he only had one leg.

After hours of struggling to remain awake, he found solace in the fact he was still alive. If it had been up to Claire, that cleaver would have found a home in his head too. He owed his life to Chloe, but even though she'd saved him, he could never be the same around her. Trusting that Chloe would be his protector for now, he allowed the weariness to win out. He closed his eyes and drifted off.

***

He opened his eyes but quickly closed them due to the bright light. *Am I dead?*

A hand touched his arm.

He squinted and saw Chloe sitting next to him. She gave him a quick wave and held up a deck of cards.

"Now?" he asked.

She nodded, an excited look on her face.

He sat up, rubbed his sore eyes and yawned. His mind raced, thinking about the events yesterday, and for a second he wondered if it all had been a nightmare.

Chloe shuffled the deck and handed out exactly seven cards each.

"Go Fish?" he asked.

She nodded.

"What time is it?"

Putting her cards down, she flashed ten fingers.

"Ten in the morning?"

She nodded, picking up her cards.

"I'm hungry. Is there breakfast?"

She jumped off the bed and brought over a tray. On it was toast smeared with butter, scrambled eggs and what could only be canned corned beef hash.

He picked up a piece of toast and took a bite. He chewed a few times before stopping. Thoughts of Kevin came rushing in. Here he was eating toast and playing cards and his friend was dead, murdered in the cruelest way. Losing his appetite, he put the toast down and pushed the tray away from him.

Chloe held up her board. *TWOS?*

He stared at her. *How can I play, knowing everything I know?*

She put the board closer to his face.

Kevin's last words came to him. He needed to know. "What's in the barn?"

She lowered the board, furrowed her brow and shook her head.

"Why did Claire kill Kevin? Tell me," Paul begged.

She wiped the board, wrote and held it up. *NO TALKING. PLAY.*

"How can I play after what happened? I need to know. Please tell me," he urged with pleading eyes.

She shook her head and tapped hard on the board. *NO TALKING. PLAY.*

"I'll play if you tell me why," Paul bargained.

Chloe clenched her jaw tight, threw her cards on the bed and stormed off, slamming the door behind her.

Paul heard another door slam shut farther down the hall. An impulsive idea popped into his head. He tossed the sheet off and lowered himself to the floor. The short distance to the door seemed like a mile, but if he was going to make an escape, now was the time. It took four hops to make it to the door. He opened it and looked out. No one was there. He listened. *Where's Claire?*

Across the hall was Kevin's old room. He needed the truck's keys and they had to be there, he hoped. Looking at the distance, he'd have to hop five to six times to reach the door. He took a deep breath and began. When he reached the door, he celebrated briefly. He turned the knob and slowly opened the door. On the dresser he spotted the keys; fortunately for him they were close. He hopped over and grabbed them. His leg was throbbing from all the exertion and he'd only gone a short distance. He still needed to get downstairs and outside to the truck. So far, everything was going smoothly.

He hopped out of the room and to the top of the stairs. The twenty-three steps represented his greatest challenge, but he had no choice, there was no other way to get down. He firmly took hold of the railing and hopped one step at a time. On the fifth step, his foot slipped. He steadied himself but dropped the keys. He squatted down, looped his finger through the key ring and stood up. He took hold of the railing and was about to step when a voice called out.

"Hi, Paul. Where are you going?" Claire asked, looking up at him from the landing below.

"Just get out of my way. I'm leaving. I won't tell a word, I promise, just please let me go," he begged.

"I can't do that," Claire said.

"You can, please."

Claire looked past him and smiled. "I told you, Chloe. He doesn't really care about you."

Paul looked behind him to see Chloe was there, tears in her eyes.

"Chloe, I need to leave. Please let me go. You're a sweet person. I'll come back. I just need to go."

Chloe rolled her hands into fists and stepped down to just above Paul.

Seeing the anger on her face, Paul continued to

plead, "Chloe, please let me leave."

She didn't reply, she only stared.

"This is a bad idea. Help me back up. How about we play some Go Fish? Huh? What do you say?" Paul asked, deciding to change course with hopes she'd forgive him.

Still she didn't reply.

"I'll play as much as you want, I swear. I won't try to leave again. I'll play any game you want me to, deal?" he begged.

The anger left her face and the tension melted away from her body. She smiled and nodded.

"Thank you."

"You can't trust him," Claire snarled.

Chloe looked at Claire, nodded, turned her attention to Paul and, without hesitation, shoved him hard.

He lost his balance and fell backwards. He slid to the bottom and smacked his head against the wall. He tried to get up, but quickly the darkness came and with it a loss of consciousness.

CHAPTER SEVENTEEN

THE FARM, EAST OF TYHEE, IDAHO

JUNE 18, 2020

In and out of consciousness Paul went until finally he came to. He was back in his bed. His head and back hurt, but his good leg was burning with pain.

The door opened and Chloe walked in, holding a tray. She set it down and waved.

Paul looked out the window. It was morning, so he'd been out for almost a day.

HUNGRY?

"Yes."

She tucked several pillows behind his head and helped him sit up. She placed the tray on his lap and took a seat on the bed next to him.

On the plate were two fried eggs, potatoes and toast. His stomach growled at the sight of the food.

She held up her board. *SORRY.*

Giving in to his fate for now, he planned on playing along. "No, I'm sorry. I won't do that again. Plus, I'm not sure if I can. I must've really hurt my leg in the fall."

She smiled.

Paul devoured his food. A question popped in his head. One that he needed answered. With a mouthful of food, he asked, "Kevin said something about…the barn."

Chloe's smile melted away.

"Chloe, is there something in the barn? Kevin seemed really upset, scared even," Paul said before pausing. "He said you were dangerous. I would agree with him concerning Claire, but you, you're not like her."

Chloe looked down, her long bangs covering her face.

"Tell me, what's in the barn?"

She shook her head.

"You can tell me, we're friends," Paul said, placing his hand on hers.

"Nothing is in the barn," Claire blurted out, emerging from the shadows of the hallway. She walked up to Paul's side. "How do you feel?"

"A bit out of it. You put me on some type of painkiller, it feels like. And my good leg, I think I hurt my knee. Feels like I tore a tendon or something," Paul explained.

"I don't think so," Claire said.

"Why do you say that?" he asked.

Claire looked at Chloe and smiled.

Chloe returned the same smile.

Paul looked beyond the tray and noticed something was different. He shoved the tray to the side and lifted the sheet and looked down to discover the most horrific thing. His other leg was missing. "My leg. You cut off my other leg? Why, why would you do that?"

"Because you promised you'd stay and play with Chloe. The only way I could guarantee you'd hold up your end of the bargain was by making sure you had no chance of ever leaving again," Claire explained.

"No! What have you done to me?"

Chloe took his hand and gave him a big smile.

Disgusted and angry, he ripped his hand from hers and screamed, "You're fucking monsters, both of you. How dare you!"

Claire pursed her lips and said, "I suggest you tone down your attitude."

"I won't. What's next? You'll cut off my arm?"

"Maybe."

Chloe reached for Paul's hand again, but he gave her the harshest look and yelled, "Don't you dare touch me. You're a fucking monster. I hate you!"

Tears burst from Chloe as she ran out of the room.

Claire stood up, her face red. "I told you I'd kill you if you hurt my sister."

Getting a grip on his emotions, he cautioned, "No, don't do that, please, I'm sorry. I'm in shock, clearly."

Claire walked to the chest of drawers on the other side of the room, opened the top drawer and removed a knife. She turned back and said, "You were warned."

"No. I'm sorry, please."

Knocking on the front door echoed up the stairs.

A look of surprise washed over Claire's face.

Knowing this was an opportunity to get rescued, Paul called out, "Help me. I'm upstairs. Help! Help!"

Claire marched over to Paul and held the knife inches from his face.

"Hello!" a woman called from out front. "Anyone home?"

She took the napkin from the tray and shoved it into his mouth.

Chloe appeared in the doorway.

"I need you to watch over him. Make sure he doesn't say a word," Claire ordered, handing Chloe the knife before leaving the room.

Heavier banging on the door. "Hello! We saw your signs. We need help."

Immediately after killing Kevin, Claire had gone out and placed the signs up again.

***

"Please, my friend needs assistance. Is anyone there?" the woman called out.

Claire reached the ground floor and peeked out a side window. On the front porch was a middle-aged woman and a man who appeared injured, his arm bleeding badly. She went to the front door and hollered, "Is it just you two?"

"Oh, thank God someone is home. Yes, it's just us. Please open. We need help," the woman replied.

***

Upstairs, Chloe held the knife with both hands, keeping her eyes glued on Paul to make sure he wouldn't do anything.

***

"One second," Claire said and ran off to the kitchen. She returned with the now infamous cleaver. She unlocked the door and stepped clear of the open doorway. "Hello."

The woman dragged the man across the threshold and beelined for the couch. "One of those things grabbed his arm. I think they might have dislocated it too."

***

In a show of defiance, Paul spit out the napkin.

Chloe approached and pointed the knife at him. The look on her face was determined.

"I like you a lot. You're like the little sister I never had. You're very sweet, but your sister isn't. We, you and I, need to leave this place, and the one way we can is to let those people downstairs know."

Chloe jabbed the knife in the air, motioning for him to put the napkin back in his mouth.

"I'm going to call out. Please don't stab me," Paul said.

Chloe stepped up and placed the knife against his throat. Her hands were shaking badly.

"You're a good and sweet girl; you won't hurt me. I trust that," Paul said.

***

Downstairs, the woman tore off her companion's shirt

and began to examine him, looking for more wounds. "I need a first aid kit; do you have one?"

Claire didn't reply. She stood back, clenching the cleaver behind her back.

***

"I trust you. You're good and sweet, you won't hurt me. I know it," Paul said, tears welling up in his eyes. "Help! Help me. They're holding me hostage!" Paul yelled.

Chloe's shaking hands got worse, and she mouthed NO.

"Help me. I'm upstairs. They're holding me hostage!" Paul screamed.

***

The woman turned, looked up and saw Claire holding the cleaver. "What are you doing?"

Claire brought the cleaver down hard on top of the woman's head. She pulled it out and slammed it against the man's throat. Blood sprayed everywhere, much of it covering Claire's floral dress, arms and face.

***

Hearing the confrontation, Paul cried out, "No. God, no!"

Chloe kept the knife at his throat, her hands trembling.

Defeated, Paul moaned and whimpered as tears flowed down his face.

Claire opened the door and stepped into the room. In her right hand she held the cleaver, dark blood dripping from it. Her piercing blue eyes stood out more against the contrast of her bloody face. "Chloe, come. We have to clean up. You know how Mother hates a mess."

Doing as she was ordered, Chloe left the room.

Claire walked up to the bedside and looked down on Paul. "You killed those people."

"No, you did. You're a monster," Paul cried.

"I'm a monster? No, I'm a survivor," Claire said. She turned and left Paul sobbing uncontrollably. She walked to the dresser, opened the left drawer and removed a long syringe. She marched back and stood above him.

"What is that?" he groaned, frozen in fear.

"It will help you sleep," she answered, sticking it in his arm.

"Why are you doing this to me? Why?" he mumbled as he drifted off.

She leaned over him and said, "Just remember, I warned you."

CHAPTER EIGHTEEN

THE FARM, EAST OF TYHEE, IDAHO

JUNE 19, 2020

Paul coughed. He opened his eyes but found he was surrounded by total darkness. The next thing that hit him was the awful smell. He wasn't in his bed, that was for sure, but where was he?

His arms were bound and tied around a slender pole behind him. He could touch the floor; it was concrete. *Where am I?*

Loud bangs came from feet away.

He jumped and his heart raced. Something was there with him.

A door opened behind him and chased away the dark.

Able to see, he looked around. To his left and right were metal bars. *I'm in a cage in…the barn.* He screamed in his mind. "Who's that? Who just came in?"

Chloe walked up and waved.

Claire came just behind her and stopped. She towered over him. "Hi, Paul."

"I'm sorry, okay. Please forgive me. I'll do whatever you say. I'll be the best playmate Chloe has ever had. I swear."

"I told you what would happen, but I'll give you one

more chance," Claire said and turned to Chloe.

Chloe frowned and shook her head.

"No, Chloe, please. I'm so sorry. Please forgive me," Paul pleaded.

Chloe scribbled *I FORGIVE YOU.*

Paul burst out crying, thinking she had changed her mind concerning his fate. "Thank you. I promise I'll be better. Please let me out of this cage. I'm scared."

She wiped the board and wrote some more. Done, she held it up. *BUT I DON'T LIKE YOU ANYMORE. YOU ARE MEAN. GOODBYE.*

"No, I'm not mean. I promise I'll be better, please," Paul begged.

Chloe walked out of sight, only Claire remained.

Banging and chains rattled in the far corner of the large cage.

Paul looked all around. He was enclosed in a large cage and something was in there with him. "What's that noise?"

Claire walked to a lever and placed her hand on it. "You said you wanted to know what was in the barn. Paul, I want you to meet our mother." She pulled the lever. A loud thud followed.

Paul first heard the footsteps; then he saw…HER.

Mother emerged from the darkness. She was a feral and, by the looks of it, hungry. What clothing she had on barely clung to her body, and what was exposed was covered in feces, blood and scabs. She cocked her head and stared at Paul with her bulging eyes.

"Hi, Mother," Claire said.

Mother looked at Claire and shrieked.

"We've been taking care of her since she changed. We don't have it in us to kill her even though Chloe wanted to after she killed Daddy. That's when she stopped talking, if you didn't know. That was a horrible day."

"No, please don't, no," Paul cried out.

Mother slowly moved towards Paul, her head bobbing up and down and her teeth chattering, making the most terrifying sound.

"Chloe, please, no," Paul begged.

Mother ran up to Paul and grabbed him by the neck, her long thick nails digging in. She leaned close and stared into his eyes.

"Since she became this way, we've been feeding her strangers that decide to wander by. This way it saves our food supply," Claire explained. "Mother seems to have a real taste for human flesh."

Mother tightened her grip on his neck.

Paul groaned in pain.

"Go ahead, Mother, you can eat now," Claire said, turning away.

Mother let out a screech just before coming down on his face with her open mouth.

Paul wailed.

Claire exited the barn with Chloe. "Sorry, baby sis."

Chloe shrugged and walked off towards the house.

Claire closed the barn door.

Paul's cries lasted for another minute before going silent.

EPILOGUE

THE FARM, EAST OF TYHEE, IDAHO

JUNE 26, 2020

Claire thumbed through a cookbook, fretting over what to make for dinner. "Do you like potpie?"

Chloe nodded.

"Oh, I know, what about pasta puttanesca?" Claire asked.

Chloe shrugged.

"It's a simple pasta dish, spaghetti, tomatoes, garlic…"

Chloe nodded and rubbed her tummy at the same time.

"It does sound good, doesn't it?" Claire said.

Chloe wrote on her board. *MOTHER?*

"I checked, the signs are still there. No one is coming by. I know she's hungry. I wish I knew what to do," Claire complained. They hadn't had a visitor since Paul was given to Mother, meaning she hadn't eaten since.

"Someone will come by soon, I just know it," Claire said, getting up from the dinette table. She walked to the counter and began to set up her dinner prep.

Knocking at the front door. "Hello!" a woman's voice called out.

Claire turned to Chloe and smiled. "See, like I said,

someone will come by soon. Now go hide. Do what we always do."

The obedient sister, Chloe ran off.

Claire took off her apron, straightened her clothes and adjusted her ponytail. She practiced smiling and even said *hello* in the mirror.

"Hello, anyone here?" the woman called out from the front door.

Claire stepped to leave but stopped when she realized she'd forgotten one thing. She opened a drawer and pulled out the cleaver. With her favorite weapon in hand, she went to the front door. Before opening it, she peeked out.

The woman wasn't alone. Two other women and a man were with her.

"Who are you?" Claire asked through the door.

"We need food, water, shelter," the woman answered. "Do you have any? The signs said you do."

"We do. Can I trust you?" Claire asked playing the part.

"You can. We mean you no harm," the woman said.

Not worried, Claire unlocked the door, opened it and stepped aside.

The woman followed by the others came inside and looked around curiously.

"Hello," Claire said, extending her right arm and keeping her left behind her back, holding the cleaver.

"Hello, nice to meet you," the woman said, taking Claire's hand and shaking it.

"What can I help you with?" Claire asked.

"Like I said, food, water and a place to sleep. We've been on the road. It's hell out there," she replied.

The others gathered in the living room leaving only Claire and the woman in the foyer.

"We can help you with that," Claire said.

"We? So you're not alone?" the woman asked.

"No, I'm not alone. Oh, by the way, my name is Claire."

"Hi, Claire, my name is Sabrina and this is Ashley and Trent," Sabrina said pointing at them. "And she is Natalie, a new edition to our group. We picked her up a few days ago outside of Twin Falls."

Natalie waved and said, "I've been so lucky lately, I come to Idaho for some needed vacation time and the world ends. I thought I was going to die then these guys helped me, now we find you and you're charming farm house." Natalie looked carefully at some trinkets on a small table. "These look like antiques."

"They were my mother's, she collected," Claire said.

"I used to buy and sell rare items before, not much use for that now," Natalie said.

"Thank you for opening your house," Sabrina said.

"You're very welcome. Glad we can help," Claire said, closing the door.

"Are your parents here?" Sabrina asked, taking off her backpack.

"Just me and my sister, Chloe," Claire said carefully placing the cleaver in a drawer without anyone noticing.

Trent walked over to the fireplace mantel and ogled some of the framed pictures. "Is this Mom? Wow, she's hot. I would have loved to meet her," he joked, holding up a picture of Mother while making inappropriate facial gestures..

Disgusted by his comment, Claire marched over and ripped the picture from his hand. "We don't disrespect Mother." Claire made sure to keep the cleaver hidden behind her back by pivoting away from the others.

"Sorry, I was just joking; plus it was really a compliment, who doesn't like—"

"Enough, Trent," Sabrina scolded.

Holding the picture tenderly, Claire walked towards the kitchen, "Maybe you'll get a chance to meet her."

"What did you say?" Sabrina asked.

Claire stopped, turned and said, "I said dinner will be served soon. I hope you like pasta puttanesca."

THE END

DETOUR

ABOUT THE AUTHOR

G. Michael Hopf is the best-selling author of THE NEW WORLD series and other apocalyptic novels. He spent two decades living a life of adventure before he settled down and became a novelist full time. He is a combat veteran of the Marine Corps and a former executive protection agent.
He lives with his family in San Diego, CA
Please feel free to contact him at geoff@gmichaelhopf.com with any questions or comments.
www.gmichaelhopf.com
www.facebook.com/gmichaelhopf

DETOUR

BOOKS by G. MICHAEL HOPF

THE NEW WORLD SERIES

THE END
THE LONG ROAD
SANCTUARY
THE LINE OF DEPARTURE
BLOOD, SWEAT & TEARS
THE RAZOR'S EDGE
THOSE WHO REMAIN

NEW WORLD SERIES SPIN OFFS

NEMESIS: INCEPTION
EXIT

THE WANDERER SERIES

VENGEANCE ROAD
BLOOD GOLD
TORN ALLEGIANCE

ADDITIONAL BOOKS
HOPE (CO-AUTHORED W/ A. AMERICAN)
DAY OF RECKONING
DRIVER 8: A POST-APOCALYPTIC NOVEL
LAST RIDE

G. MICHAEL HOPF

Made in the USA
Middletown, DE
19 November 2019